BLACK BULLET
PURGATORY STRIDER

6

SHIDEN KANZAKI

ILLUSTRATION BY
SAKI UKAI

"Just three seconds. Make them count."

BLACK BULLET 6
CONTENTS

BLACK★BULLET

PURGATORY STRIDER

SHIDEN KANZAKI

ILLUSTRATION BY SAKI UKAI

YEN ON

NEW YORK

BLACK BULLET, Volume 6
SHIDEN KANZAKI

Translation by Nita Lieu
Cover art by Saki Ukai

This book is a work of fiction. Names, characters, places, and
incidents are the product of the author's imagination or are
used fictitiously. Any resemblance to actual events, locales, or
persons, living or dead, is coincidental.

BLACK BULLET, Volume 6
©SHIDEN KANZAKI 2013
All rights reserved.
Edited by ASCII MEDIA WORKS
First published in Japan in 2013 by KADOKAWA
CORPORATION, Tokyo.

English translation rights arranged with KADOKAWA
CORPORATION, Tokyo, through Tuttle-Mori Agency, Inc., Tokyo.

English translation © 2017 by Yen Press, LLC

Yen Press, LLC supports the right to free expression and the value
of copyright. The purpose of copyright is to encourage writers
and artists to produce the creative works that enrich our culture.

The scanning, uploading, and distribution of this book without
permission is a theft of the author's intellectual property. If you
would like permission to use material from the book (other
than for review purposes), please contact the publisher. Thank
you for your support of the author's rights.

Yen On
1290 Avenue of the Americas
New York, NY 10104

Visit us at yenpress.com
facebook.com/yenpress
twitter.com/yenpress
yenpress.tumblr.com
instagram.com/yenpress

First Yen On Edition: April 2017

Yen On is an imprint of Yen Press, LLC.
The Yen On name and logo are trademarks of Yen Press, LLC.

The publisher is not responsible for websites
(or their content) that are not owned by the publisher.

Library of Congress Cataloging-in-Publication Data
Names: Kanzaki, Shiden, author. | Lieu, Nita, translator. | Ukai, Saki, illustrator.
Title: Black bullet. Volume 6, Purgatory strider / Shiden Kanzaki ; illustrations
by Saki Ukai ; translation by Nita Lieu.
Other titles: Purgatory strider
Description: New York, NY : Yen On, 2017. | Series: Black bullet ; 6
Identifiers: LCCN 2015046479 |
ISBN 9780316304993 (v. 1 : pbk.) | ISBN 9780316344890 (v. 2 : pbk.) |
ISBN 9780316344906 (v. 3 : pbk.) | ISBN 9780316344913 (v. 4 : pbk.) |
ISBN 9780316344920 (v. 5 : pbk.) | ISBN 9780316344944 (v. 6 : pbk.)
Subjects: | CYAC: Science fiction. | BISAC: FICTION /
Science Fiction / Adventure.
Classification: LCC PZ7.1.K29 Blac 2016 | DDC [Fic]—dc23
LC record available at http://lccn.loc.gov/2015046479

ISBNs: 978-0-316-34494-4 (paperback)
978-0-316-34501-9 (ebook)

1 3 5 7 9 10 8 6 4 2

LSC-C

Printed in the United States of America

BLACK BULLET 6 CHAPTER 03

HOTARU KOURO

1

It was with an overwhelming sense of chagrin that Shigetoku Tadashima, inspector from Magata Station, eyed Atsuro Hitsuma as he opened the interrogation room's door. Tadashima nonetheless gave his direct superior from police HQ a dutiful salute.

"How are things going?" Hitsuma asked, pushing his glasses up the bridge of his nose with his middle finger.

"Well," the barrel-chested Tadashima replied, "why don't you see for yourself?"

On the other side of the room's one-way mirror, they could see an elderly man in the interrogation room, answering questions. His face was darkly tanned, and his hair was a salt-and-pepper mix. The puffiness of his face made his eyes appear deeply sunken in their sockets. Tadashima knew through years of detective experience that a person's personality and life experiences were often written on their face, and judging by this man's, he surmised the man had led a tough, hardscrabble life.

"Who's he?" Hitsuma inquired.

"Yuuki Iwama. Fifty-six; taxi driver. An eyewitness said he let a couple who looked like Rentaro Satomi and Hotaru Kouro into his cab, so we have him in for questioning at the moment. He swears he doesn't remember taking a fare from anyone like that."

"There's no kind of record on the taxi's computer about where he went, or when?"

"Turns out he didn't have one," Tadashima replied. "It looks like his taxi firm engages in some pretty drastic cost cutting in order to keep their fares the lowest in Tokyo Area."

"What's your gut telling you about him, Inspector?"

"Ah, he's probably got *something*."

Hitsuma crossed his arms together. "Do you think we can get it out of him?"

"He's just a person of interest at this point. We can't press him too hard. But did you visit the apartment with the body yet?"

"I stopped by for just a bit. It was…a *heartbreaking* scene." Hitsuma shook his head in an expression of sorrow, but his words rung hollow, like an unpracticed actor reading a script for the first time.

After all, the word *heartbreaking* tended to be thrown around a lot, in contrived displays of empathy.

Tadashima had been first on the scene. The high-rise apartment complex that Gastrea forensic pathologist Ayame Surumi called home was the picture of hell itself, the survivors breathing wild tales of tire-shaped monsters attacking them. The police had found two of the wheeled machines as they cased the place, both with its innards destroyed. He shook off the thought before his mind could flash back to the grisly sights that remained tattooed to the backs of his eyelids.

"The doctor Rentaro Satomi visited was killed in her bathroom," Tadashima began. "She had been dead for a fairly long period of time, so he couldn't be the guy for that one. Immediately after, those crazy machines started their building-wide rampage—and, once again, Rentaro Satomi started coming to people's rescue.

"What I really don't get, though, is the body in the elevator. We found it in the car after the cable snapped and it fell to the second-level basement. It was so badly dismembered that we haven't been able to get an ID yet, but the body had some kind of electronic parts infused within it. I mean, this is crazy. Why are there all these bodies wherever Rentaro Satomi goes?"

"What do you think, Inspector?"

Tadashima looked up to find Hitsuma gauging him carefully, his face serious. Tadashima felt something cold behind that stare as he tried to assemble his thoughts.

"It's pretty clear to me there's some nonpolice entity pursuing him. What I don't understand is what kind of motive Rentaro Satomi could possibly have. Given that they made contact with Dr. Kakujo posing as the victim's relatives, they must have some kind of mission or goal in mind. They might even be trying to clear their name, for all I know."

"......"

"Do you think it's time," Tadashima continued, deliberately trying to fight off Hitsuma's eerie silence, "that we made this a public investigation?"

"We can't do that," Hitsuma replied, his tone indicative of how ridiculous the idea was to him. "The news already reported that Rentaro Satomi fell off the Magata Plaza Hotel and drowned in the river. If people find out he's been shrugging off police pursuit and skipping around Tokyo Area scot-free this whole time, it's going to be an absolute embarrassment. All we have to do is secretly arrest him and say that we plucked him out of the river earlier."

That's "all" we have to do? Tadashima found himself wondering. Hitsuma, whether he knew of the inspector's doubts or not, turned his eyes to the one-way mirror, taking in the interrogation.

"This would be a lot easier," he whispered in a monotone, "if that cabbie would just tell us what he knows already."

His release from police custody ultimately had to wait until two in the morning.

The moment taxi driver Yuuki Iwama left the front entrance, he was greeted by the sticky summer night air. The high humidity raised his discomfort level off the charts. Brooding over his stressful day, he turned the car's ignition. They said they'd let him know if they needed anything else, but given how they had acted, they'd no doubt be calling his company's office again soon. He was exhausted to the core and not particularly enthusiastic about running a night shift now, so he simply drove home instead.

He texted his wife as he did, figuring there was a chance she was still awake. No answer. To him, it was both a disappointment and a relief. It was easy for him to imagine the torrent of questions she'd unleash once he confessed where he'd been. She may have been the love of his life, but there was no way he could reveal who had climbed into his taxi hours earlier.

Soon, he pulled up to his home, in a quiet neighborhood outside the main city. His eyebrows arched up as he did. The lights were on, and he sensed there was activity inside. He pulled into the driveway to park the car in the garage, wondering what she was doing at this time of night.

Then he noticed that the lawn mower was still out in the yard. That wasn't normal. His wife was so picky about that sort of thing. The moment she spotted so much as a speck of dirt on the kitchen floor, out she came with the dustpan and broom.

The door was unlocked, emitting a soft creak as he pushed down on the lever to open it. The front foyer was littered with shoes and mud tracks, as if something heavy had been dragged through.

It was like…like someone had attacked his wife while she was doing yard work and dragged her inside. *Wasn't it?* Yuuki cursed his own overactive imagination as he reached back outside and pushed the doorbell. A pair of shrill tones echoed across the house.

There was no response. No, hang on—he could just barely hear something coming from the living room down the hall.

His pulse started to race, his breathing quick and shallow. There was no doubt in his mind that something bad was going on. He grabbed the ceramic flower vase by the front door, spilled out its contents, and held it by the neck to use as a weapon. He didn't bother to remove his shoes as he stepped back in.

As he approached the living room, he realized that the sound was muffled groaning. Once he was at the doorway, Yuuki resolved himself, then jumped into the room.

The sight shocked him.

"Izuho!"

His wife was lying on the living room floor, hands and legs bound with tape, blindfolded and gagged. She looked like the cocoon of a bagworm moth as she groaned.

Yuuki ran to her in a panic, only to find his arms restrained from behind and something sharp and cold pressed against his neck. A knife blade, probably.

"Don't turn around," a low, threatening voice intoned. His body tensed up, sweat running down his forehead.

A home invasion?

"Who—who are you...?"

"I could tell you," the voice replied calmly, "but if I did, there'd be no saving you or this woman."

It was clear from the tone that the owner of the voice was uninterested in further questioning along these lines.

"I want to ask you one thing. Where did you drop off Rentaro Satomi and Hotaru Kouro?"

This is no robbery at all. This guy's in pursuit of that freaky civsec pair. Yuuki was too intimidated to make any kind of reaction.

"You have two choices," the voice continued. "Give me the location, or give me the location after I hurt you."

"After you hurt me...?"

"I'll start with the nails. Twenty of them. Not yours—the girl's. Once I'm done with that, I'll take off the fingers next. You can speak up anytime if you feel like talking."

Yuuki let the vase fall out of his hand. It shattered loudly against the floor. He shook his head, not minding the shallow cut the knife made against his neck. Tears poured from his eyes.

"No... Stop. Anything but that."

"Okay. So you know what you have to do, right?"

In his mind, Yuuki brought his hands up to Rentaro's. *I'm sorry. I'm truly sorry.*

"District 18. Nagatoro City. The illegal-immigrant slum."

"Right."

The knife lowered, and the darkness behind him lessened.

A sharp silence descended as he gingerly looked over his shoulder.

Not a trace of the home invader remained.

The moment Yuuki realized he was safe, he immediately fell to his knees on the floor.

After what seemed like the millionth investigation meeting at Magata Station, Hitsuma was eating a not so palatable catered box lunch when the phone rang. Looking at the name, he stood up, walked to an empty part of a nearby hallway, and answered it.

"Swordtail? Why didn't you go through Nest? Is it *that* important?"

"I found out where they got off the taxi. It's in Nagatoro City, District 18. The illegal squatter camp."

"Nice work. I'll get an operation together ASAP. Is that all?"

His conversational partner, for some reason, was oddly silent. After a moment, though, he continued, his voice low and emotionless.

"Is it true Hummingbird got killed?"

Hitsuma hesitated for a moment.

"...Yes."

"Well, it figures, what with how she swaggered around all the time. Pfft. Wish she realized how much work this put on me *before she went off and died like that."*

"You better watch yourself, too. This isn't any normal job."

"No worries."

Hitsuma stared at his phone for a few moments after the call ended. If his next move failed on him again, he'd have no choice but to deploy Swordtail himself. He didn't want to go that far—not for a single target like this—but he nonetheless had zero doubt that the man would make short work of Rentaro Satomi and his accomplice.

He walked back to the office snickering to himself, carefully hiding the smile of joy trying to make its way to his face.

2

Rentaro Satomi, together with Hotaru Kouro, passed through the curtain together. "Thank you!" a voice shouted.

Back at the public bathhouse, all the lights were out. It was dark, shockingly so if your eyes were used to the light, but the stars in the sky helped to light the pathway ahead. His entire body felt comfortably warm as he noticed Hotaru looking at him, cheeks flushed red after the bath.

"That wasn't bad," she said. "I was wondering why you wanted to visit the bathhouse out of nowhere."

"Yeah," he breathlessly replied. "I'm glad it was up to your standards, Princess."

To him, as long as he didn't think about his current circumstances too much, walking under the stars down this path devoid of people was almost...fun. Refreshing.

He checked the time. Two a.m. His shirt had shrunk a bit after he washed it at the laundromat next to the bathhouse, and he tugged at it uncomfortably as he stretched out his torso.

Hotaru's ripped tank top had been stitched back together with a sewing kit. There were still bloodstains on it, but the wash had faded them to the point where you wouldn't notice unless it was pointed out.

It had only been about seven hours since the intense confrontation they'd had with Hummingbird in the apartment. Rentaro couldn't exactly settle down for a nice bath with all the raw wounds on his body, so he had to wait until no other customers were around and be satisfied with rubbing a wet towel against himself to get the sweat and dead skin off.

But he was still in decent enough shape. The gunshot wound in his left leg, caused by a ricocheting bullet during the Hummingbird battle, had been fully taken care of, and the bullet removed. Walking, at least, wouldn't make it any worse. Normally he'd rush right over to a hospital instead of jerry-rigging his own treatment like this, but as a fugitive from the law, the health system had little to offer him right now.

"You never took a bath with Suibara or anything?"

Hotaru flashed a resentful look. "Why do *you* care? Are you...? Rentaro, did you actually share the bathtub with your own Initiator?"

Rentaro, bewildered, scratched his head awkwardly. "She kept pestering me about it until I said yes... Damn it, I *knew* other civsec pairs didn't do that. She tricked me!"

Hotaru sighed and gave Rentaro a commiserating nod. "Rentaro, you should really watch how you act in public. You're pretty well-known for stuff like needing a ten-year-old girl to get off, and walking around town at night with a pair of panties on your head, and things like that."

"Things like... Wait, what?"

Hotaru turned aside.

"Hey, why're you averting your eyes like that?"

She remained silent, her countenance uneasy. Rentaro was about to ask another question, a particular and unfathomable fear dawning on him, when someone walked past them.

He had a feeling the person was watching them. Before he knew it, his heart froze over.

Rentaro took out a pair of sunglasses from his pocket and put them on, then slipped a glove over his Super-Varanium artificial hand, shining a dull black in the starlight. He'd purchased a pair of gloves after conferring with Hotaru and deciding he should at least hide his face and hands in public.

Yesterday, Rentaro took the girl along with him to Shidao University Hospital, where Dr. Kakujo pointed them to the apartment of Gastrea pathologist Dr. Surumi. That was where Hummingbird decided to strike at them. He still had no idea how Hummingbird had picked up on their movements, but one plausible theory was that someone had spotted him out on the street and reported it to the authorities.

Another possibility: security cameras. Whenever one of the countless surveillance cams scoping out Tokyo Area spotted a Gastrea, an embedded algorithm would use cues like heat-radiation patterns to identify the type and send alerts to all civsec officers in the vicinity. A few modifications to the software code behind that system, and it'd be entirely possible to have the cameras search for specific faces—or eyeball patterns, for that matter—to identify a person.

In both of those cases, sunglasses would have an immediate defensive effect. But—

"Dahh! I can't take this!"

Rentaro ripped the glasses off. Wearing sunglasses at night wasn't much different from putting on a blindfold. He'd bump into things, making him seem even more suspicious to passing strangers than if the glasses were off. Hotaru didn't care much about this, however: "Being dressed in all black like that makes you suspicious-looking enough already," she'd said curtly when Rentaro had brought it up.

He and Hotaru were on speaking terms again, at least, but Rentaro still had some lingering discomfort about their clash during the Hummingbird battle.

—"I told *you*. *The only reason I'm working with you is so I could hunt down the enemies after your blood. You've been the best decoy I could ever have hoped for. If you think we've got some kind of partnership going on, let me assure you, it's all in your head. I always hated you, anyway.*"

—"*If you're so hell-bent on saving people's lives, why didn't you save Kihachi's?*"

She must have picked up on the current awkwardness between them, too. Whenever she talked, she kept it short. Every time, it seemed to end in an awkward silence. And when that happened, all they heard as they walked down the shuttered shopping area was the sound of their own footsteps. It was hard to say how long the most recent silence lasted before she finally opened her mouth once more.

"You know," she began, "when I brushed you off and went upstairs, everybody up there was already dead. They must've all had parents, and families, and brothers and sisters, too." She shook her head. "I had no idea there are people out there who can...*do* that. Without a second thought."

The events in that building must have given her something to think about.

"Yeah, so you see, then?" Rentaro said. "Those are the types of guys we're fighting against."

As he thought about whether saying any more would be prudent, he heard the sound of a faraway siren ripping through the silence. The pair immediately looked at each other. Hotaru, at least, responded instantly, looking into the night sky as she focused her hearing to discern where the siren came from.

Gradually, they could hear it echoing closer and closer: the now-familiar sound of a police cruiser.

Rentaro and Hotaru slipped into a narrow alleyway behind a nearby building, breathing silently as they kept themselves hidden. It smelled like oxidized oil.

Before long, two of the dreaded police cars whizzed by the alley. Taking a moment to crane their heads around the corner, checking to make sure the police didn't make a U-turn, the two then stepped back onto the street.

The cars were gone, it seemed. They didn't seem like the typical patrol—they were going too fast for that. Maybe it was some other crime in progress.

"My hideout's in that direction."

Rentaro gulped.

"No way."

The denial seemed to ring hollow as the portent of Hotaru's observation wriggled its way into his brain. If her suggestion was correct, coming directly home after this would be a singularly bad idea. It might just be his current guilt complex writ large, but right now, they couldn't afford to take any chances. All that awaited on the other side of that risk was their arrest, followed by an inescapable guilty verdict.

"Are there any tall buildings around here?"

"No, but… Here, let me go look."

Before Rentaro could say anything, Hotaru's eyes turned a crimson red. The next moment, there was a blast of wind—and she was gone. Looking upward, he spotted her atop one of the arched streetlights that lined the asphalt at regular intervals.

This flustered him. Even if this *was* a deserted avenue in the middle of the night, there were still cars sporadically passing by. If one of the Cursed Children was spotted in a town like this, there'd be at least one or two people screaming in a panic before long. That would drive more people to come out, and after that, there'd be no more defusing the situation.

Hotaru, whether aware of that or not, pointed forward. "I don't see them yet," she intoned. "Let's get a little closer." Then, with another dartlike leap, she was atop the next streetlight. Rentaro opened his mouth to protest, then closed it again, resigning himself to his fate as he followed along.

This tense march down the street continued for a few moments— until Hotaru suddenly stopped. Rentaro realized what it was immediately. The glass-lined building in front of them was awash in dull, red, flashing lights. Reflections from police cars, no doubt. Not just one or two, either.

Hotaru came back down to Rentaro, heels clicking softly against the pavement.

"I saw them."

"No dice, huh?"

She shook her head. "We better abandon that hideout. It's dangerous here."

Rentaro shivered. He was the one who suggested visiting the bathhouse, growing increasingly sick of the dingy, cramped bathroom at home. It wasn't a decision he brooded over for particularly long before making it. But, by sheer coincidence, that decision had a profound effect on their fates. If they had been at home, they'd absolutely be subject to soul-withering police interrogation right now.

The two backtracked on their previous path. There was no destination in mind. They just had to get out of there.

But both had made the mistake of focusing on the police force behind their backs. Now they could see another police car—reinforcements, maybe—coming toward them. It didn't have its siren on, so by the time they noticed it, it was already disturbingly close.

Ducking into an alley would be all but telling the cops they were suspicious. Rentaro took Hotaru's hand. Hotaru gave a surprised look, but she quickly picked up on his intentions. She gripped his hand tightly.

"Just keep it as natural as you can."

From the corner of his eye, he saw Hotaru nod. The police car in front of them, its exhaust pipe making a soft sound, was no more than twenty meters away. He found himself turning his eyes downward.

The headlights illuminated their bodies from the chest down. The sound of tires scratching against the pavement as the car moved on sounded unnaturally loud to their ears. For some reason, the car was on the shoulder of the road, slowing down as it drove by. Rentaro lowered his head farther down as the car finally passed them.

Is it going?

As the two continued walking, they could hear the sound of the tires stopping on the pavement behind them, followed by a door opening and closing.

Rentaro closed his eyes. *God help me.*

Taking a lightning-fast look behind him, he could see two police officers walking their way, flashlights in hand.

"Excuse me! Couple over there."

Rentaro pretended not to hear, trying his hardest to keep his pace naturally slow and his legs from shaking. Using a finger, he suggested turning into a nearby alley. They hadn't discussed this at all yet, but their movements were still the picture of elegant efficiency.

"Hotaru!" Rentaro said, the moment they were in the alley and out of police sight. She gave a nod in response, then brought her hands around his shoulders.

"Hang on."

The next moment, he felt an explosive shock wave across his entire body, the g-forces that lifted him up making him feel like his organs were being twisted apart. With Rentaro's body in tow, Hotaru unleashed her full force, leaping against the sides of looming buildings to ascend. Rentaro's eyesight lurched from one direction to another, almost causing him to bite his tongue.

He didn't immediately faint on the spot once they reached the roof because of the supersonic speeds he had already experienced at the hands of his usual Initiator.

Looking down, they spotted the two officers walking around the alley, dismayed at not finding them there. He pulled back, trying not to make a sound, and gauged the situation as a lukewarm wind hit his face. Before long, the cops would radio in this potential sighting of Rentaro Satomi and Hotaru Kouro, and the entire block would be crawling with police. They needed to head out ASAP.

"That taxi driver must've blabbed about where we were," Hotaru whined in an uncharacteristically gloomy tone. The thought occurred to Rentaro the moment he realized their hideout was discovered. He had deliberately put it out of mind.

"Even if he did, that's our fault."

If they'd wanted to, they could have either threatened or bribed the driver to keep quiet. But they hadn't. Rentaro trusted him, and so did Hotaru. No matter what happened or didn't happen to them, the responsibility for it all came down upon themselves.

"It's sad, though."

"Yeah."

Their eyes met. Hotaru emitted a lonely smile, eyes sparkling. Rentaro could feel his pulse grow heavy. This was an Initiator, a person who walked the fine line between little girl and grown woman, between human and Gastrea. How could she show off such a…*threatening* smile?

Rentaro averted his eyes, just to make sure her face didn't enthrall him any more than it already did.

Turning the knob, Rentaro opened the metal door. It creaked loudly in protest.

The cheap flashlight they purchased from a convenience store was proving to be worth even less than the pittance Rentaro paid for it. It took the combination of its feeble beam and Hotaru's phone backlight to fully illuminate the area around them.

The walls were white in the otherwise featureless room, as were the two columns in the middle of the large chamber. The floor, made of marble and feldspar, was even whiter. Rentaro attempted to move a pile of unused stone to sit on, only to be rewarded with a choking fog of white dust. He regretted forgetting to buy an anti-dust mask when he was at the store.

"*Koff-koff*... Well, this ought to work."

They had checked to make sure this sculpture studio was abandoned before going in. Rentaro closed the rusty shutter of the window, cutting off the moonlight. The room grew even darker, adding to its horror-film atmosphere. The eeriness unnerved him a little, but he resolved to put up with it. If any light from the flashlight made its way outside and someone reported it, they'd have to find yet another place to take shelter for the night.

Rentaro sat down, resting against a column as he propped the flashlight on the floor. Hotaru, seated next to him, gave a frustrated scowl.

"I can't sleep like this. There aren't even any pillows."

"Just be glad we got a roof over us, okay?"

They had naturally considered checking into a hotel, but—after extensive debate—decided against it. The police weren't that stupid. Once they realized Rentaro wouldn't be coming back to their hideout, they'd send people to hit up all the hotels in the region. They might already be disseminating wanted posters to all the front desks in a ten-minute radius. They couldn't just waltz into *that* flytrap.

"So what're we gonna do now?"

"Well..." Rentaro strung the words together as he stared at the floor. "I'm wondering about that Gastrea corpse with the star marking on it.

I know defeated Gastrea get processed after a certain waiting period, so it's got to be in storage somewhere or another. I was thinking we could start there."

Hotaru nodded.

"Um, also...about that assassin we faced, Hummingbird..."

"Yeah, I was thinking about her, too," Rentaro said. "She had the same five-pointed star at the base of her thigh. That, and she had *two* wings around it, not just one."

Hotaru opened her eyes wide. "She did?"

"Yeah."

"What does that mean, though?"

"I have no idea."

With that being the only hint to go on, they clearly had a need for more intel.

The pair spent a little more time discussing their future activities before their voices trailed off. In the silence, evening cicadas chittered here and there.

Suddenly, Rentaro felt something warm and soft on top of his left hand, which was planted on the floor. Surprised, he looked down to find Hotaru's palm above his.

"I...I killed someone."

Hotaru was small, balled up on the floor, using her left arm to hold her knees tight against her body. Rentaro watched her for a few moments. "Hotaru," he offered softly. "If you were scared to kill someone, that's your sanity giving you a heads-up. You have to make sure you don't forget how that feels. Once you pass that point, you won't be able to hold out against it any longer."

"What happens if I don't get scared anymore?"

"You won't be a person anymore. You'll just be a murderer, a barbarian seeking the thrill of carnage... I dunno. Call it what you will. But it's nothing good."

"All right. Thanks. I'll remember that."

Behind the words, Hotaru looked depressed, clearly left at a loss to break out of this line of thinking. Suddenly, Rentaro realized he was mentally overlapping Hotaru's face with that of another girl he knew. Part of the Satomi family. A ball of energy.

He shook his head, wondering what was wrong with him as he tried to keep his voice cheerful. "Hey, Hotaru, you mind if I ask you a stupid question?"

"What?"

"You called it…'enhanced regenerative skills,' didn't you?—your ability? If someone shot you in the head or whatever, you'd be dead for at least a little while, right?"

"If by 'dead' you mean my pulse would stop, my pupils would dilate, and my heart would stop beating…then sure."

"Um…so is there a heaven, or whatever?"

Hotaru's eyes were as big as saucers for a moment. Then she heaved a weighty sigh and turned her back to him. Rentaro winced.

"Wh-what?"

"Wow. That really *was* a stupid question. Nobody's ever asked me *that* one before."

That was the last thing Rentaro expected from her. But after a moment, Hotaru looked at him from the corner of her eye. "Are you religious at all?"

"No."

"Okay. I'll tell you, then. There's not. It's just like passing out. It goes all black and you lose consciousness."

"Why'd you ask if I was religious?"

"Well," Hotaru said with a self-effacing grin, "I figured you'd be disappointed if I said there wasn't any heaven. Besides, even if there was one, *I'm* sure not getting in. Heaven's for humans, right? That counts me out right there."

3

A light rain had been pattering outside the window since morning as a depressingly overcast sky dominated the scene.

The clerk's sleepy eyes suggested he'd had a late and alcohol-powered night. His puffy face indicated a history of wild partying with next-morning regrets. His lab coat was wrinkled and bent out of shape, and his unkempt hairstyle made him look old beyond his years.

"All right," said the man, introducing himself as Shibata. "So you came here this early in the morning just because you wanted to see Gastrea number 440?"

"Is there a problem with that?"

"No, not really, but... All right. Lemme see your license, please."

"Here."

Hotaru placed her license in the palm of the annoyed man. This piqued his interest for a moment: He eyed Rentaro up and down. It wasn't a written rule, but it was customary for the Promoter to provide his license in situations like these. Rentaro's, of course, was still confiscated by the Seitenshi.

"Um, I...I forgot mine at home."

"Oh. Well, the Initiator's is fine, too. Sign here, please."

Hotaru, keeping her cool perfectly, signed the papers. Then she looked ahead, Rentaro following her gaze.

They peered down the long corridor behind Shibata's shabby-looking desk chair, iron bars preventing their access. Wind echoed from beyond; it must have been getting into the dimly lit hallway from somewhere. The air ahead was chilly, too, no doubt to help preserve the corpses. Hotaru rubbed her arms for warmth.

The two had arrived at this Gastrea cadaver storage site at the crack of dawn. Sumire's university hospital had a storage depot of its own, but compared to this specialized facility, it was pretty low-key.

Shibata thrust a key into the lock and turned it. With a rusty creak, the door opened inward, and he led the pair into the corridor.

The blue LED lighting on the ceiling added to the site's overall creepiness, and the group's footsteps echoed against the hard flooring across the hallway.

Suddenly, Shibata stopped and turned to the pair. "Y'know, why do they bother with those iron bars, anyway?" he asked. "They're already dead by the time they get sent here, aren't they?"

"There've been cases in the past where a Gastrea we thought was dead revived itself, or some offspring in the womb made their way out and caused all kinds of chaos. So that's why."

Just thinking about that frustrated Rentaro. There was never any telling. A pandemic could just start in there, for all he knew.

Soon, Shibata stepped into one of the side rooms. Rentaro and

Hotaru followed. The moment they entered, they felt the air grow even colder.

It was a small room, about 150 square feet or so, and its walls were lined from top to bottom with handles. At first glance, it looked like a bank's safe-deposit vault, but each handle opened a cadaver compartment about twice the size of ones at a morgue. And inside one was the Gastrea with the star symbol that had captured Dr. Surumi's attention and ultimately led to her doom.

Rentaro watched expectantly as Shibata searched for the right box, using some notes on a piece of paper for reference. Then he turned around and beckoned to them. Hefting the handle open, he raised a hand to block his face from the intense cold inside, like opening a freezer.

Before them was a rectangular box plenty large enough to comfortably house a human being lying down. Rentaro patiently waited for the cold mist to dissipate, only to reveal—

"Huh?"

There was nothing inside.

"Hmm? Well, *that's* weird."

Shibata made an almost comical grimace as he thumbed through the documents in his binder. "Oooh, yeah, guess we were just a little bit too late. One of the processing managers came to pick it up about half an hour ago."

"Processing manager?"

Shibata rolled his eyes. "Aren't you guys civsecs? You don't know how Gastrea get processed around here?"

"Is it a problem if I don't?" an agitated Rentaro replied. The clerk winced a bit.

"Okay, so when they find a Gastrea, an alert comes out and whichever civsec neutralizes it first gets the reward, right? If it's a type we've never encountered before, we bring on a pathologist to perform an autopsy and examine its heart and brain and stuff for vulnerabilities. Once that's done, it's stored in here for a period of time. Then, every month, a processing manager comes in, picks up the bodies, and takes them away for cremation. They gotta be really careful with the incineration, too, to make sure no internal viruses survive it."

"Cremated? So they burn all the Gastrea bodies they take out of here?"

"Ninety-nine percent, yeah. Some of 'em get stuffed or used for experimentation or whatever, but that's just the really exceptional cases. Too bad you guys didn't come here sooner, huh?"

"That's..." Rentaro felt his head go hazy. Their one remaining lead had been snapped. If they hit a dead end there, they were completely done for.

"Hmm? Hang on."

Shibata, realizing something, lifted his head from the binder and gave his guests a quizzical look.

"We don't have any Gastrea pickups scheduled today..."

"What do you mean?"

"Well, I don't really know myself. The processing manager comes at a pre-scheduled day once a month to pick up Gastrea cadavers, but I guess he showed up here this morning, too. That's the first time they've ever shown up unannounced, I think. And what's more, the only Gastrea they took was the one you guys are here to examine."

Hotaru and Rentaro exchanged glances. "Hotaru," Rentaro whispered to her, "this 'processing manager' guy..."

"He's probably part of Hummingbird's group. That, or someone close to them. Either way, now we know they're busy trying to hide the evidence."

Which meant, if considered another way, getting a chance to examine the corpse would be problematic for that group. Which, in turn, meant that this star-bearing Gastrea was more valuable to Rentaro and Hotaru than ever before.

"They must know what we're trying to do by now. So they made off with the corpse unannounced, even though they knew other people would notice that. Damn it..."

Hotaru, her memory perhaps jogged by this, turned to Shibata. "Um, Mr. Shibata, does this process manager come in with a truck or something to haul the bodies out?"

"Yeah. A big one. One of those moving-van jobbies."

"And you said he came in about half an hour ago?"

Shibata nodded again.

"Could you maybe call the truck to get it back here?"

Rentaro froze.

"Like, that binder…"

Before he could finish the thought, Hotaru took the binder from Shibata's hands and showed it to Rentaro. The sheaf of papers inside included the form Hotaru signed when they first came in. It was a basic sort of visitor log, including entries for names, times, IDs or civsec-license checks, addresses, phone numbers, and reasons for the visit—a truly classic piece of government paperwork.

Hotaru's finger was pointed at the words "Nagahara Transport" recorded in the log thirty minutes prior. She must have been suggesting they contact the Nagahara Transport driver, presumably still in traffic somewhere, and order him back to the site.

"But do you think the phone number on there's real?" she asked.

"Hey, uh," the incredulous-looking Shibata interrupted, "I don't know what you guys are talking about, but—"

"I think that's probably gonna be the same person from Nagahara that always comes here," Rentaro said, crossing his arms. "Not that I saw him, but if it was some random guy coming in unannounced on a new schedule, I'm pretty sure this guard would've stopped him. But if we make contact with him, how do we get his truck back here?"

"Umm…" He watched as Hotaru dropped her head down. But just as he started to think they'd hit a wall, another thought crossed his mind:

"Well, look, more than anything else, they want to get their hands on that Gastrea with the star, right? If we said that they found *another* Gastrea corpse with a star on it, that oughta make them come back, don't you think?"

"That's *it*!" she exclaimed.

The sound of Hotaru's unexpectedly loud reaction bounced off the walls. She blushed and coughed nervously, regretting the outburst.

"…Um, I mean, yeah, that works for me."

Rentaro turned to Shibata. "Could I ask you for some help?"

Shibata winced at having the spear turned in his direction. "What? Why do I have to do that? I don't really like lying to people, and stuff…"

"Well, listen, you probably like your job to be pretty slow-paced, right?"

"Huh? My job? Well…it's a little *too* boring here sometimes, yeah, but I sure don't like it when it's real busy, either. Why do you ask?"

"If we let that Gastrea get away, thousands of people might die. The morgues are gonna be so full of *human* cadavers, they'll have to use this site for temporary storage."

Shibata's expression froze. "What…do you mean…?"

"Please. Don't ask me anything. Just help me out a little. We're not gonna be a bother to you."

A few moments of hesitation. Then:

"…All right. I don't really know what's going on, but I'll trust you guys. If y'all are pranking me this early in the morning, though, it sure ain't funny."

Then Shibata briskly sprang into action, the sleepyheaded, bleary stare from earlier now a thing of the past. Reaching for a nearby phone, he picked up the receiver and dialed a number.

"Um, hello? Is this Nagahara Transport?" he began cheerfully. "Hey, thanks for all your hard work! I'm just calling 'cause you guys showed up here earlier to pick up a Gastrea for us…? Right, right, that transport…"

Rentaro left the building, taking Hotaru along with him. The drizzle from earlier was now a barely perceptible sprinkle, albeit one falling almost horizontally in the strong winds. They noticed a trash can tumbling along the street at high speed. The weather report said the rain would die down by the end of the day—but if it was starting up *this* early in the morning, Rentaro pictured a soggy day ahead.

The two ran across the street to a coffee shop and ordered the cheapest thing on the menu. There were almost no customers. They took a table by the window, which afforded them a full view of the Gastrea morgue. Amid the rain-blotted landscape, the gray exterior of the morgue remained still, emitting a uniquely melancholy atmosphere. It was still just nine in the morning. The seconds ticked as they sat, taking in the pitter-patter of the rain as they silently drank their coffee, their boredom driving both to blankly stare outside.

They had done everything they could. Picking up a random Gastrea from the morgue, they had used the photograph they found in Dr.

Surumi's apartment as a reference to scrawl a star on its corpse in permanent marker. Compared to the photo, it was pretty clearly an inept imitation. They used a little bodily fluid to blur it a bit, just barely giving it a semblance of likeness.

Now they just had to wait.

"Feels kinda like we're in a detective drama or something, doesn't it?"

"Detective? You're a *prisoner*. That's too dumb to even bother replying to."

Rentaro's eyebrows twitched, his lips pursing. "I'm not a prisoner! I haven't even received a verdict yet."

"Ahh, same difference."

"God damn it, you…"

"Pfft."

"Pfft!"

The pair turned their backs to each other. As a date, it was a failure. Wondering why his life had to end up like this, Rentaro summoned his composure and decided to have a late breakfast. He wanted something sweet in order to keep his blood-sugar level high, so he opted for a packet of glazed mini donuts.

He was rather robotically reaching for the fourth one, sweet enough to make his teeth feel like they were going to melt, when a truck with the Nagahara Transport logo silently appeared and sidled up next to the morgue.

That was probably the one. It was manned by two people. One of them, in a gray jumpsuit, climbed out and went to the door while the other one stayed in the cab.

Rentaro and Hotaru excused themselves from the coffee shop and cut a wide path around the truck, not bothering with an umbrella. They approached it from the side, taking in the aroma of the exhaust and the sound of the idling engine. They could see the driver in the side mirror, having a smoke and listening to the radio. He didn't seem to have noticed them. Hotaru's face stiffened, but Rentaro raised a hand to stop her. This clearly annoyed her.

"Why not? There's only one of them."

"We don't know if they're the enemy yet. Let's tail them and see what they do."

From behind the truck, they approached a yellow taxi and tapped against the window. The napping driver lifted his hat off his face and sleepily squinted at them. He blinked a few times, half-suspicious of this set of customers, before pushing a button to open the back door for them.

"Where to?"

The moment he stepped inside, Rentaro pointed at the truck ahead. "That truck's gonna take off soon. I want you to follow it for me."

The driver flashed a surprised look at them. The memory of yesterday's taxi trip ending in disaster resurrected itself in Rentaro's mind. In a near daze, he made up a story to convince the driver. Whatever it was—Rentaro forgot all the details about five seconds after concocting them—it worked well enough that the still-dubious driver gripped the steering wheel and turned his eyes to the truck. The windshield wipers rhythmically swung to and fro, brushing the misty rain off the glass. Other droplets dripped down the windows, merging with one another to form larger, faster spheres.

Nobody said anything.

After a while, a large Gastrea stretcher came out of the building. The processing manager wheeled it out, a large white sheet covering it, and brought it to the truck's container. Surveying his surroundings, he knocked at the door, waiting a certain interval before each knock.

After a moment, another processing manager emerged. This made Rentaro's heart skip a beat. There were more, after all. Why was one stationed inside the container itself? As he thought about this, the two carried the Gastrea off the stretcher. It was too dark to see inside the container, but a brief glint of light made him arch his eyebrows.

"Hotaru, did you see that?"

"See what?"

"...Ah, never mind, then."

Part of him prayed it was just his imagination. If that glint was from what Rentaro thought it was, it proved that this truck's intentions were very sinister indeed.

The engine sprang into action as the truck slowly shuddered to life. The taxi followed behind, keeping a prudent distance. The light rain fell in a powdery drizzle, the mechanical, metronome-like motion of the wipers adding to the sense of emptiness inside the car. Everyone kept their attention forward, breath bated.

The taxi was a stopgap measure, but Rentaro had to admit: This was a gifted driver. Visibility through the windshield wasn't exactly high, but he did a magnificent job of not coming too close while staying in perfect sync with the truck.

Soon, they were entering an expressway—but once they passed the toll, things began to change. The truck suddenly swerved into the right lane, rapidly accelerating. Rentaro hurriedly instructed the driver to speed up, but right when he did, the truck applied the brakes.

He furrowed his brows at this behavior, only to arch them wide at the next instant. Was this the truck driver's way, maybe, of discovering any cars that might be following them? It had to be. They had cast the line, and now they were sure they caught a nibble.

Then, the next moment, the truck accelerated. This time, it wasn't stopping. It whizzed down the road at high speed, snaking its way through traffic as it gradually began to disappear from sight.

"It's getting away! Follow them!" Rentaro said, half rising to his feet. The resulting burst of speed from the taxi sent him right back in his seat. The engine roared, shaking the entire vehicle. The speedometer blew past one hundred kilometers per hour, just barely skirting the speed limit on the expressway. The resulting speed sent them back behind the truck, next to it, and then in front of it. The rain-soaked view and wet pavement were undoubtedly affecting the grip of the tires. Even a single steering mistake could have led to disaster on the road.

"I—I really can't go faster than this!" the driver finally shouted. The engine sounded like an F1 car. But thanks to his hard work, the truck was now firmly back in sight. The taxi's lighter weight gave it the advantage over a fully loaded container truck.

Rentaro instructed the driver to approach the truck's side from the left. They waited until they had an open spot for the move, but suddenly, the truck tried to run them off the road at breakneck speed. They braked just in time to avoid being sandwiched between the truck and the guardrail.

A cold sweat ran down his body. But the real fear for Rentaro came when he saw what was inside the now-open container. Squinting at the sight, he gazed in wonder. The metallic weapon he caught a glimpse of earlier was bolted to the floor of the truck, its ferocious muzzle aimed squarely at them.

It was a Browning M2 heavy machine gun: a supremely powerful, full-auto, .50-caliber rifle that even saw use in anti-tank warfare, although its primary purpose was for downing planes or penetrating armor. In many ways, it wasn't a machine gun so much as a machine *cannon*. It was *not* something a Gastrea transport company would just happen to have bumping around inside its trucks.

The enemies working against Rentaro must have fixed on to his intentions by then. They were preparing for anything and everything.

The processing manager in the container pulled the giant machine gun's cocking handle, readying it for fire, and aimed its sights squarely on the taxi.

We're dead, said the sixth sense that worked beneath Rentaro's intellectual mind.

Then the flash, and the gunshots.

The car spun out with a screech, sending Rentaro's viewpoint reeling. He was jostled in his seat, bewildered, and then he saw the taxi spin toward the concrete wall lining the highway. He shut his eyes tight.

"Rentaro!"

Suddenly, there was an impact at his side, followed by the feeling of being pushed into the air. Then, the sound of something shattering.

But there was none of the pain he expected. The wind was rushing against his cheeks, too strongly for his tastes, and the summer rain—still falling down almost sideways—beat against his body. He could hear his school uniform fluttering in the gale.

He opened his eyes a slit and was finally clued in: He was in the air. And like a piece of carry-on baggage, he was hanging off the arm of Hotaru Kouro, who was gritting her teeth above him. At the last possible moment before the collision, she had lifted herself from the car and escaped with Rentaro, too.

"We're falling," she said, interrupting Rentaro before he had a chance to give his thanks. He was suddenly pulled down by gravity, the rain-soaked pavement on the ground approaching at terminal velocity.

But before it could reach them, they rolled together onto the roof of a passing truck, shrugging off the impact and just barely slipping right off the edge before steadying their balance.

The damage to his semicircular canals made Rentaro's head spin to the point of nausea. He tried his hardest to gain a grasp of his situation, raising his head upward.

He had thought they were on top of the enemy's truck for a moment, but they weren't. That truck was overtaking the cars in front of them at high speed in the rain, all but laughing at them as it sped away.

Instinctively, he took a look behind them. "How's the taxi driver?!"

"Look in front of you! You're gonna die!"

Rentaro closed his eyes for three seconds, just enough time to keep him from falling into panic mode. Mentally, he forced himself to switch gears. "Hotaru!" he shouted. "Can you reach that truck by yourself?"

"I can't do that! It's going one hundred and thirty kilometers an hour!"

Being atop a truck of their own, they were forced to scream at each other. The intense rain and strong wind were lowering both of their core temperatures. Their clothing was completely soaked.

Why couldn't Enju be around at a time like this...?

Looking ahead, the enemy truck was still gaining distance on them. The gunfire was gone. The rain was blocking their visibility, as it did for everyone else, and they must've opted to hold their fire. But if they got too close to the truck, that could change.

What do I do?

"Okay, Hotaru. Can you carry me and start jumping to other cars?"

Hotaru gave him a stupefied look for a moment, then—after another moment of thought—nodded lightly and stood up on the container truck's roof.

"I can't go that far at once."

Rentaro stood up with her. He was greeted by torrential rain and a wall of air pressure from in front. It took everything he had to keep from falling off as he wrapped his arms around Hotaru's stomach from behind. She turned halfway back at him—and then, with a steely resolve, jumped. They landed on the roof of a black van up ahead, then leapt over to a sedan passing the van on the right. So it went, one after the other, as they caught up to the enemy truck at breakneck speed.

Rentaro was deeply agitated. The wind and rain were one thing, but if she misgauged a single jump, they would both be battered against the pavement and sustain major damage. But Hotaru's outstandingly nimble moves, all executed at hair's-breadth timing, came at an accuracy that could only be described as transcendent.

Hotaru Kouro had an innate sense for this, just like Enju. A sense that could never be cultivated by any normal person.

"I see it!"

Squinting through the curtains of rain from behind her shoulder, Rentaro could see the red of the van's taillights. But it also meant they were in firing range again. In fact, the person manning the gun—spotting the pair of pursuers he was so sure were out of the picture—expressed clear surprise as he leapt for the gun and swung it around.

The anxiety made Rentaro's blood vessels tense.

"Here it comes!"

An intense barrage of flashes came as the bullets from the Browning tore through the porous concrete in front of their car like a pile of dirt. The holes forced the vehicle to swerve, and left ugly scars on the road.

But Hotaru wasn't out to lose. Even nimbler and more accurately than before, she leapt from vehicle to vehicle. The .50-caliber Browning gunfire, missing them by an instant, instead thudded through the engine block of the previous car, triggering an explosion. With a screamlike screech, it spun out and off the road.

With superhuman skill, Hotaru continued her leapfrog act. The heavy machine gun traced her path in the air, turning her footholds into scrap one by one. The unending torrent made the rain evaporate in midair, with Hotaru and Rentaro threading the needle in between. A bullet brushed by Rentaro's cheek at supersonic speed, making a *twing* sound as it did—but all he could do was fight off the g-forces tugging at his body, gritting his teeth until they were nearly in pain.

"There's too much fire! I can't get close!"

Finding herself running short on footholds to jump on, Hotaru was rapidly cornered. The rows of cars behind them were a pockmarked hellscape.

Rentaro's mind raced, trying to find a solution—then the sight before him drained the color from his face.

"Hotaru! Tunnel!"

The tunnel through the low hill in front of them was no more than three and a half meters tall. They couldn't execute any flying leaps in there—and once that advantage was taken from them, they were dead.

This is it, thought Rentaro as he shut his eyes tight.

But then, like a bolt of lightning, an idea ran across his brain:

"Hotaru, can you run on the ceiling?"

Hotaru shot him a look, mouth agape. But she must have grasped the question a moment later, because she turned forward again, jaw determined.

"Just three seconds. Make them count."

The rapidly approaching tunnel entrance loomed, looking like the hideous maw of a demon roaring in laughter.

With a loud *whoosh*, they were in. For just a moment, the curtain of rain lifted, clearing the scene around them. The machine gun swiveled and locked on to them. But Hotaru jumped just a blink in advance.

Immediately afterward came gunshots, followed by an explosive shock wave. But they didn't look back. They didn't have time to.

Ignoring the scene behind her, Hotaru leapt up and landed on the ceiling, running horizontally across it.

"Rentaro!"

Now upside down, Rentaro released his hands from Hotaru's mid-section and—as if swinging on a flying trapeze from his feet—took a position inverted from the ceiling. His hands free, he gripped his Beretta handgun and held it up—or down, in this case. The truck was in his sights. He quieted his breathing, closed his eyes—and unleashed his eye. A geometric pattern emerged in its iris, performing calculations at lightning speed. The hems of his clothing flapped impatiently in the wind, all but expressing the panic within Rentaro's own mind.

Look at what you did, you bastards. All those civilian victims.

Seeing Rentaro size him up with the look of an enraged beast, the enemy gunner must have been scared witless. His whole body trembled as he tried his best to turn the gun's muzzle toward him. But it was too late.

Rentaro fired three times. He was aiming next to the gunner—at the rear left tire.

The moment the hole opened in the nitrogen-stuffed tire, it immediately burst, the high inside pressure seeking an escape. The truck lurched, its driver misjudging his steering, then collided against the right-hand tunnel wall. He had applied the brakes, but the force of nearly 120 kilometers an hour against the wall lifted the truck up into the air, sending it to its side and spewing metallic shrapnel on the ground as it bounced and rolled another thirty meters or so. The gunner was thrown clear of the vehicle, striking the ground.

But Rentaro, from his less-than-ideal firing position, was facing some recoil of his own. It was one thing for a lightweight Initiator to run across the ceiling. It was quite another for her to support Rentaro's weight at the same time.

Just as the floaty feeling of being thrown by something flashed back to his mind, he found the asphalt down below rapidly approaching his head.

He balled himself up, taking the impact at the top of a shoulder as he bounced up into the air. Pain seared across his brain as he was sent spinning off by the force.

Ensuring he was no longer in motion, Rentaro shakily pulled his body up, hands on the road as he tried to keep from ejecting the contents of his stomach. With unsteady steps, he ran toward Hotaru, who had fallen from the ceiling in similar fashion.

"Hotaru! Hey, Hotaru!"

He kneeled down and slapped her cheek. She must have fallen head-first. There she lay on her back, fresh blood dampening the side of her head. She was motionless.

After repeatedly calling for her, Rentaro saw Hotaru's eyelids blink a few times then groggily force themselves open.

"You are so stupid. I can regenerate myself, remember? I'm a lot more solidly built than *you* are."

Rentaro breathed a sigh of relief.

"That's not the problem," he said, "you idiot."

Because she healed faster than most, she failed to realize that the sight of a wounded child lying on the ground was what concerned Rentaro.

"What about the van?"

He turned around, startled. "I'll check it out," he said, picking up the Beretta on the ground before advancing slowly on the vehicle. It was on its side, now blocking all lanes of the tunnel. The traffic behind it was stopped, the chaos on the other side already clear to his ears.

One of the jumpsuited processing managers was hurt and bleeding from his head. The other two were bruised and dazed but not seriously injured. After a crash as spectacular as that, Rentaro was surprised nobody was killed. Only one was conscious, and just barely, but the injuries would prevent resistance for the moment.

Going around back, he found two Gastrea corpses thrown from the rear of the chilled container.

Finally found you.

There was the Gastrea that he drew the fake pentagram on, and next to it, the Gastrea in the picture he'd found at Dr. Surumi's home.

It was an impressive sight. At nearly six meters long, its extended proboscis made for an eerily eye-catching silhouette. It had wings like an insect, its rib cage exaggerated and basket-shaped. Rentaro couldn't guess what biological elements clashed against one another to create this.

"That's definitely the one Kihachi and I killed a month ago," Hotaru said, clearly put off by the Gastrea at her feet.

This was what started this whole mess in the first place. When Dr. Surumi discovered the star marking on this Gastrea and conducted an autopsy—she found something. And that something erased both her and Suibara. There had to be something on this Gastrea body that linked it to the Black Swan Project, still a total mystery to Rentaro. It *had* to, or else it'd be the end of the road for him.

Snapping on the nitrile-rubber gloves that he borrowed from the morgue, Rentaro ignored his sense of disgust as he examined the stomach area, the surgical scar easily noticeable across it. When he opened the incision, he was greeted by a sharp, acrid stench that permeated deep into his eyes, battering his mucous membranes and making him turn his face away.

But there was no time to linger. The police must have known by then about the gunfight on the expressway. He needed to wrap this up in around two minutes if he wanted enough time to flee.

So he stuck his arm in. Through the thin layer of rubber, he could feel the slippery flesh around the stomach on his fingertips as he brought the heart into view. It was the whole, translucent organ, like the innards of some giant squid—and the star mark he was seeking was right nearby.

He removed his knife from his waist. Slowly, carefully, he cut out a square of surrounding tissue and put it inside a film case he had along with him. He also took a sample of the epidermis, the outer skin layer, just in case.

The squishy heap and its samples were already decomposing on him. He thought about, and simultaneously dreaded, the idea of ducking into a nearby grocery store for some dry ice. But he still had some other business to handle.

Moving to the driver's side of the truck, he opened the door and grabbed the still-conscious processor by the collar, setting him down on the ground. He had a cut on his cheek, a bloodstain on his jumpsuit at chest level, and a look of sheer animosity in his eyes as he silently glared upward.

"You got nowhere to run," the man warned.

"Where were you going to take this Gastrea?"

The processor did not reply.

"Why did your group try to take the Gastrea away?"

The man was silent.

"What's the Black Swan Project?"

"......"

"*Answer* me, you asshole!"

The anger was clear in his voice as he lifted a fist into the air. Something grabbed at it.

It was Hotaru, and she was shaking her head.

"It's time."

His temper made him fail to notice, but if he strained his ears a little, he could hear the sirens. Rentaro gave the jumpsuited man another vengeful glare. There was so much he wanted to ask him, but it wasn't like he could kidnap him and run. *Damn* it.

"Where to next, Rentaro?"

Rentaro brought the film case up to Hotaru and lightly shook his head. "We need access to a facility where we can have this tissue sample analyzed," he said, his voice low. "I dunno if it's something any old lab could help us with, but there's one person I think we can count on."

He took one more half turn toward his prisoner.

"Relay a message to Hitsuma and Dark Stalker for me. Tell 'em I'm gonna get Enju, Tina, *and* Kisara back."

Then he turned back ahead and fled with Hotaru.

4

Tsurayuki Kimishima tightened his jaw, checking the sturdiness of his stool as he sat down on it. He had been silent for three hours already, his eyes transfixed on the floor.

Suddenly, a pair of hands slapped down on the steel desk in front of him.

"Look, will you just *talk* already? Huh? How long d'you think you can get away with that?"

The tiny room they were in made the body of the detective, his crew cut making him look the very picture of a high-school gym instructor, seem to loom even larger than normal. The passing shower had grown stronger, making the humidity in the interrogation room intense.

Tsurayuki lifted his face slightly from his jumpsuit, stained with blood and soot. "I'm using my right to remain silent," he steadfastly said. "Get me a lawyer. I'm not saying anything until then."

It was a more than effective way to apply further fuel to the detective's anger.

"What's with that *attitude* you got? Huh? Do you have any idea what kind of situation you're in right now? That gunfire you and your pals sprayed all over the expressway *killed* people. Why was there a machine gun mounted on your truck in the first place? Where did you obtain that from? Where were you going to take the Gastrea bodies?"

The detective glared at Tsurayuki, crawling back into his shell of silence. He found himself drawing his lips back in anger—perhaps a perverse smile at the futility of it all.

"All right. Once I'm done raking your ass over the coals, I'm tossing you into lockup. I hope you don't miss the outside world too much, because you ain't gonna be breathing fresh air for a while."

Two soft knocks came from the room's single door.

"Feh," the detective spat out as he stood up and stormed to the door. "Who is it *now*?"

And then:

"Oh, hello, um…!"

Suddenly the detective seemed intimidated. Tsurayuki looked over, wondering what was up.

"But…," he continued. "But that'd…" Then he fell silent.

Tsurayuki was left alone in the interrogation room for a while, but when the door opened again, someone new stepped inside.

It was a younger man with a long face, adorned by a pair of silver-framed glasses that gave him an air of intelligence. He had to be a detective if he was in there, but who was he? The suspense made Tsurayuki swallow nervously as he looked up.

The man stopped in front of him, then suddenly spread his arms wide.

"I'm here to protect you."

The man before him rolled up his suit and the shirt sleeve underneath. On his upper arm was a five-pointed star, three of the points adorned with ornately designed wings.

A shock ran across Tsurayuki's spine. He shot to his feet and bowed.

"Please pardon me, sir! I wasn't expecting a three-wing in here."

"My name is Atsuro Hitsuma. Don't worry. There's no surveillance in this room."

"How are my friends doing?"

"They're undergoing treatment at a hospital. Under police observation, of course. Tell me what happened."

"Y-yes, sir! I managed to burn the two Gastrea at the last minute before the police could seize them…but they took a tissue sample from it."

"Where do you think *they* went?"

"They're getting closer to the plan. I'm sure they'll look for someplace where they can analyze that sample. A lab facility as high-level as that…"

Hitsuma steeled his eyes behind his glasses.

"Shiba Heavy Weapons?"

Getting out of the car, Tadashima used his suit jacket as an umbrella, scurrying through the rainstorm toward Magata Station. He ignored those around him as he thundered into the building, his

pace quickening as he passed right by the office with the specially assigned investigation team he was supposed to be leading.

Instead, he went straight under a sign reading CRIMINAL AFFAIRS. It was quiet, devoid of detectives at the moment. They were all out pursuing leads in the Rentaro Satomi fugitive case.

Once it became clear to everyone that Rentaro Satomi was alive, the investigation team, previously figuring they'd be disbanded before long, reverted into a hive of activity. Now they had another incident to cover—a messy crime scene covering a fairly hefty stretch of freeway.

Hitsuma was just on his way out of the interrogation room.

"Superintendent Hitsuma! What'd you do with the suspect?"

"He'll be put in custody at the main HQ for the time being, Inspector."

"What?" Tadashima groaned. "Sir, with all due respect, that's complete bullshit! The taxi driver's in critical condition. We've got four people dead, shot by that heavy machine gun. I couldn't even tell you how many casualties there are. It's like a goddamned field hospital right now, where they were taken to. I have no idea what's going on here. For the sake of the victims, at the *very* least, someone needs to pry open the suspect's mouth with a pair of pliers—and that's *my* job, sir! Let me through, please!"

"That's a commissioner order, Inspector."

The response came point-blank. It put Tadashima over the edge.

"Superintendent, you know as well as I do that I'm not one to talk when it comes to ignoring orders…but what you're doing right now is textbook interfering with a police investigation! What are you trying to do, deceiving the commissioner like this? Please, sir, I want to be on your side here, but…"

Hitsuma did not answer. He simply looked down at him with a cold, lifeless stare. Looking at those eyes, Tadashima could feel the full depth of the chasm that now yawned out between them. Even if the entire world turned upside down, there would be no changing his mind any longer. That was all too clear now.

Tadashima spun around. "We're done working together. I'm taking action on my own from now on."

"We were told by the investigation headquarters that we are to operate as a two-man team. If you decide to take action on your own volition, I reserve the right to report that to my superiors."

"*You're* the one acting on your own volition! If you don't like it, feel free to rat on me or punish me or whatever you like."

Tadashima started walking—right out of the police department. He never looked back. Hitsuma, watching him go, made sure he was firmly out of sight before sighing and shaking his head.

"We have to get rid of him now," said a new voice. "Otherwise it's just gonna get worse."

Somewhere along the line, Dark Stalker—Yuga Mitsugi—had sidled up next to him. The operative shot a sharp glance at Tadashima.

Hitsuma shook his head again to stay him. "No. If my partner gets killed, I'd have to personally answer to that. Leave him. We're acting just as shady as he is."

With effort, Yuga relaxed his gaze and shrugged. "So what's the plan then, Mr. Hitsuma? 'Cause this isn't really going too well right now, is it? Like, three of our members arrested for a mass shooting?"

"It won't be a problem," Hitsuma said as his middle finger propped up the bridge of his glasses. "The two unconscious suspects in the hospital are going to go into cardiac arrest. We're planning to have Tsurayuki Kimishima write a note in his cell and hang himself. No leaks, no nothing."

"Not a stone left unturned, huh?"

"Not a one. You make a mistake, you pay for it."

"If you seriously want to eliminate Rentaro Satomi, you need to use me."

"The decision's already been made. He's been assigned to Swordtail. You're on standby."

Yuga gave him a cold, sideways glance, then silently disappeared down a station hallway, sulking.

There was no doubting his skills in battle, Hitsuma thought to himself, but there was something unfathomable about Yuga still; it was hard to read what he was thinking at any given point. In the end, it was easier to control a pure, unadulterated warrior over someone with a few threads dangling loose.

It was eight in the evening. Glancing outside, he saw that the skies, spitting rain since the morning, were finally starting to clear up. It was going to be a humid night.

5

The rain lifted as darkness began to entwine itself around the area, the occasional streetlight sprouting off the ground drawing a spotlight through the black.

Rentaro, Hotaru in tow, peeked up from behind a wall, peering into the open space in front of him—or, rather, a certain section of it.

"Neat, huh?"

"It's like some kind of samurai mansion..."

From over the mud walls that encompassed the property, they could see the roof of a three-story building that looked straight out of a samurai drama. In fact, it seemed like someone had purchased the remains of some shogunate-era manor and moved the entire thing to use as a private residence. It was home to Miori Shiba, daughter of the head of Shiba Heavy Weapons.

Shiba was commonly known as a key supplier of weapons to the police and self-defense force. It was also involved with leading technical research in a wealth of fields, from electronic devices to ballistics calculation and DNA analysis for police investigations. And yet here was this house, going well beyond a penchant for Japanese aesthetics and looking more like a stubborn refusal to face modernity.

It was clear, at least, that Miori's fondness for traditional Japanese styles was not just an odd quirk on her part but a policy upheld by her entire family. And the main question now was how they were going to find Miori in this massive complex and convince her to help them out.

As a fugitive from the law, he doubted he could expect a friendly welcome when he rang the doorbell. Quite the opposite, in fact. Rentaro craned his head up again, tracing the wall's perimeter with his eyes. Then he ducked back down, finding exactly what he was expecting up there.

"People, huh?"

"Yeah. People."

There was a car near the front gate, positioned to be as inconspicuous as possible. It wasn't a black-and-white patrol car—a sight Rentaro was beyond tired of—but he guessed it was probably still the authorities.

If the front gate wasn't happening, it was time to find a weaker spot they could prod.

"I'll go on ahead," Rentaro said. "Could you just take me to the top of this fence?"

"No, I'll go. Why're we trying to convince her, anyway? Let's just kidnap this Miori woman and make her do our bidding."

"Wh-what?" a bewildered Rentaro replied.

Hotaru snorted at him. "I'm just saying, it'd be a lot quicker to break out some firepower and make her bend to our will. That's how it works with the targets I've beaten up until now, anyway."

"Yeah, right. You think I'd ever let someone as unstable as *you* near Miori?"

"...Look, I don't know what kind of idea you've got about me, but I'm just trying to handle this in the best way possible, using the best means possible. And if *my* way's the most efficient, then what's the problem?"

Rentaro wanted to bury his face in his hands.

"Look, there's no guarantee Miori would listen to *you*, but she'll listen to *me*, okay?"

"Glad to see you're so confident about that. How about a little friendly competition, then?"

"What in the world are you—?"

Suddenly, a pair of hands grabbed his body, and he was seized by a violent acceleration as the ground fell out from under him.

When his feet felt terra firma again, they were on top of the fence.

"Get down."

He followed Hotaru's lead, falling to his hands and knees without having any idea what he was doing. He could hear the clacking of ceramics underneath him, the dampened *kawara* roof tiles rubbing against his stomach.

Up there, they could see the wide entirety of the Shiba residence in one fell swoop. The sight made Rentaro temporarily forget his mission with an appreciative sigh.

Below him, stone garden lanterns lit darkened pathways at regular intervals, leading to a square gazebo. The gazebo was perched atop an island in the middle of a large pond that dominated the central area of the property. Traditional washbasins were located here and there along the walkways, too, and a number of buildings dotted the paths, adding spice to the view wherever he looked.

The Shiba family was living in the midst of an imperial Japanese garden. But it was more than just simple beauty. Surveillance cameras were whirring left and right at strategic locations throughout, and Rentaro could see a security officer or two patrolling the premises.

"Let's see which one of us can find Miori first. If I do, I'll make her do our bidding *my* way. It's the same thing in the end, right?"

Hotaru stood up on the fence before Rentaro could stop her, then soundlessly dashed across the tiled surface.

Rentaro was both stunned and disgusted. He knew this alliance— between a girl burning for revenge and a civsec stupid enough to fall into the trap he was in—was on thin ice from the start. It was a team of convenience for both sides, and every now and then, it was bleedingly obvious that they lived in completely different worlds. As long as revenge was all she lived for, he supposed she wouldn't even bother taking notice of how many good intentions and would-be ideas she'd trample over along the way.

What a menace I've teamed up with, Rentaro thought. There was no way he could leave Miori in her hands.

Not, of course, that he had any idea where Miori was. He sized up the property once more, his mind at an impasse. It was 8 p.m. Common sense indicated to him that the family was either at the dinner table or enjoying an evening bath. It chagrined him to think of it, but Hotaru—zooming right for the main building—very likely had the right idea.

Come to think of it, Miori had confided in him once that the intensity of her schedule—school, practice, the private after-school learning center her parents made her go to—was seriously getting on her nerves. It had been a rare moment for her usual free-wheeling self to complain like that, and it stuck in his mind because of it.

She had confessed to having a home tutor, as well as private instruction in the traditional arts of folk dance, the *koto* harp, and archery. Miori's parents seemed intent on meticulously quashing any time the girl could possibly have to herself. The stress must have made her drop her guard around him—that one time, at least.

...*Archery?*

A thought occurred to Rentaro as he scanned the property. Soon, he found what he was looking for: a dilapidated structure, really nothing but a horse barn compared to the splendor of the main residence. A bit beyond it, he could see a pair of targets lined up, the little *kasumi-mato* used in Japanese archery. They were too far away to be distinctly visible.

He considered this for a moment, then nodded to himself. There were about eight meters between the fence top and the ground, but leaping off the steeply sloped roof that topped the mud-stone perimeter fence would take no small bit of courage. He sidled down and sat on the edge, legs dangling.

Then all of a sudden, one of the wet tiles came loose underneath him. Rentaro swung out for a handhold but missed the structure entirely. He scrambled to hang on but felt a sudden sense of weightlessness instead.

The dark of the ground came upon him too quickly to incite fear. He planted down on the dirt, a shock wave crossing his spine and going all the way to the top of his head. Still, just barely managing to stay on his feet, he instantly found a darker shadow hurtling toward him from above. Rentaro threw his hands above his head just in time to catch it.

Even though the roof tile that fell with him had the grace not to shatter and reveal his position, the experience was still greatly embarrassing. It really would be pitiful if he was discovered in such a pathetic state.

Just then, a nearby animal's snarl hit his ears, and Rentaro froze.

It was the third piece of the security puzzle, after the cameras and the guards.

Cursing himself for not noticing it when he was still safe, Rentaro wiped the sweat from his brow and turned toward the sound.

Their eyes met, revealing to Rentaro a pile of reddish-brown muscle giving him a supremely masculine glare despite the difference in species. Its head was wedge-shaped, its ears cropped but still bolt upright in the air.

The watchdog of Shiba Acres gave another ill-foreboding growl.

A Doberman pinscher.

...*That* part of the complex wasn't very traditional.

Security would be there soon. No time to waste. His adversary kept its rear end bent, ready to pounce if an attack appeared imminent. Then with a growl, it lunged, aiming straight for Rentaro's neck. It was exactly what he expected, which made both dodging it and landing a chop against the base of the dog's throat not terribly difficult.

Rentaro dragged the limp Doberman to the nearby woods, where he hid, too. Right on cue, a security guard ran up to the scene. Rentaro held his breath, assessing the guard from the dark, tall grass. A flashlight beam whizzed past him, the brightness making him blink. The guard restlessly shook his head and, after a moment, sighed. "Right," he said to nobody, maybe embarrassed about getting worked up over a false alarm, as he disappeared from view.

Rentaro let out a broad sigh of relief, then proceeded along, keeping himself hidden among the lines of pine trees as he took a wide turn around the pond and toward the archery range.

The canola oil burning in the stone lanterns emitted a bittersweet aroma, the flame flickering in the wind and slightly altering the shape of Rentaro's shadow as it let out a thin sort of warmth. Perhaps the residents were holding some kind of party inside, because the wind brushing his cheek brought with it the sound of cheering and old-style Japanese court music.

Finishing his arc around the pond, he poked his head up from behind a stone, finally able to take in the range ahead.

With a light *thunk*, an arrow buried itself in one of the targets in the distance.

Someone was there.

Clearing away the rain-glistened reeds before him, Rentaro bent down and carefully approached the range from the rear. There was another whoosh in the air, followed by the sound of something thudding into something else. His eyes, now used to the darkness, clearly saw a girl on the other side, the white of her archery uniform visible in the night.

She had a chest protector on, her bow drawn as she stayed alert. It was a very elegant pose, and the sweat glistening on her face made it all the more alluring to him.

But her expression through the dimly lit air was less than content. It was like she was practicing her skills in order to shake off some nagging doubt in her mind.

"Staying pretty active in this heat, huh?"

"Who's that?!"

He raised his hands into the air to show his innocence. There was no artificial lighting in the range, despite the late hour. Her eyes must have been just as used to the dark as his.

She gave a look of surprise, followed by a gasp.

"My dear Satomi? Are you the real thing…?"

"Do I look like a fake?"

Rentaro expected this to be followed up by her usual silliness. Probably along the lines of *At* this *time of night? Were you trying to sneak in my room for a little hanky-panky? Oh,* such *an honor,* or the like. But with another whoosh, something thudded just past his side.

Rentaro stopped; looking aside, he saw the shaft of a duralumin arrow vibrating in the air, practically in front of his nose.

"They said you were dead," Miori whispered, shaking as her hands clutched the bowstring. "You have no idea how worried I was."

Shocked, Rentaro felt deadly ashamed of his lackluster self-introduction. As far as the TV news was concerned, he had either drowned or bled to death near the Magata Plaza Hotel. That would explain the look of confused discontent he had seen on her face all the way across the archery range a moment earlier.

"I'm sorry I made you worry."

There was a twinge of pain in Miori's downturned eyes.

"Satomi… Satomi dear, did you really…really…kill him?"

"No!" he replied instinctively, only to draw back and weakly shake his head. "I don't know if you'll believe me or not, but I've been framed. Will you give me some time to explain myself…please?"

Miori nodded silently, beckoning him to continue. So Rentaro gave a quick summary of everything that had happened to him thus far—the bizarre request from a familiar client; the client's subsequent assassination; his arrest and escape; the girl he was working with now; and the mysterious Black Swan Project they were trying to blow the door open on.

By the time he was done, a look of supreme relief was clear on Miori's face.

"Guess you never had it in you to kill in the first place, hmm?"

Rentaro stuck his hands in his pockets and pouted. "What'd you think?"

"Hey, did you hear, though, my sweet Satomi? I heard a rumor saying Kisara's gonna get married soon."

A wave of pain, similar to a strike against his head with a hammer, coursed through Rentaro.

Kisara? Marrying?

"To whom?"

"Uh, someone named Hitsuma from the police."

Him—

The rage was enough to practically add a red tint to his eyesight. The possibility should have been obvious to him long ago. He had thought his foe sent Enju to the IISO, Tina to jail, and the Tendo Civil Security Agency into de facto oblivion because he feared the strength of their Initiators. He was wrong.

"I keep on calling and texting Kisara, but she won't respond to anything I give her. You know what's up with that, Satomi?"

The distressing mental image of Hitsuma ravaging Kisara flickered into his brain. It nauseated him. He hung his head, eyes closed tightly as his fists began to shake.

Kisara...

I want to see them. Everything else can wait. I want to rescue Enju, and Tina, and hold them in my arms. I want to rescue Kisara, and apologize for all the horrible things I said to her. Then everything could be normal again—

"I..."

"...Oh, were you busy?"

Hotaru chose this moment to speak up from her perch atop the roof over the bow stations. Working her way to the ground, she sidled up to Miori.

"Who's this?" Miori asked her.

"Hotaru Kouro. I'm with this guy. We kind of have a few common goals." Then she looked at Rentaro, as if that was all the explanation she felt she owed the girl whose property she was on. "The archery range, huh? You got me there."

"Heh. Yep. I found her first. So hands off."

Hotaru raised her hands up, eyes closed in surrender, and shrugged.

"Um, so what's this about?" Miori asked Rentaro. "Is this the girl you said you were working with?"

He thought for a moment before responding. "Miori... Thanks for telling me about Kisara's marriage. But I can't go see her yet."

He fished around in his pocket for something that felt smooth and cold in his hand, and showed it to Miori. The film case was packed with dry ice, ventilation holes on the top of the cap.

"There's tissue from a certain Gastrea inside this case. It's almost certainly linked to this whole frame job. I need access to a lab where we can analyze it."

Gripping the steering wheel of the black Mercedes-Benz, Rentaro adjusted his position in the seat beneath the belt and tensed his body. It had been a while. Trying to remember everything he learned at driving school, he checked the signs around him and pushed down on the accelerator. The car awkwardly lurched forward.

Given how this was his first shot at driving a vehicle as relentlessly fancy as this, he couldn't be blamed for a few butterflies.

"A civsec license lets you drive pretty much anything, hmm?" Miori bouncily observed from the passenger seat.

"Don't talk to me. If I hit something, it's gonna be your fault."

"Promoters can drive anything except tanks and fighter jets," Hotaru added from the rear, her head the only part visible from the front seat. "If you're an Initiator, though, all that license gets you is anti-corrosion drugs. It's pretty useless."

"Sounds pretty nice. Maybe I should score one of those."

Rentaro took time from intensely focusing on the road up ahead to snort at Miori. "It doesn't come *that* quick, you know."

Miori, who had taken a moment to change into a kimono before leaving, opened up her hand fan and covered her mouth as she fanned her face. "I just figured, anything *you* have, *I* should have, too. See what I mean, Satomi dearest?"

"Ugh."

"I think the fact that someone on Rentaro's level can score a license so easily says a lot about the whole system, too," Hotaru added.

"Are you guys *trying* to start a fight with me?"

"Oh, turn right, here."

Rentaro half swerved at Miori's command, barely making the turn.

"So where're we going, anyway?" he asked a moment later.

"Shiba Heavy Weapons HQ."

The light turned red ahead. The car quietly decelerated. Rentaro found himself checking the rearview mirror to make sure nobody was following them. When they took the Mercedes out of the property, they asked Miori's normal chauffeur to take out the limousine she used for commuting to school as a lure for the detective parked out front. He had taken the bait—the Mercedes had made it out of the premises without a hitch—but now was no time to let their guard down.

A digital clock stood out clearly against the neon blur of the cityscape before them. It was approaching 10 p.m.

Before long, they spotted a building just a little bit taller than the rest of the glowing, dazzling edifices around it. He expected it to be mostly abandoned at this time of night but was surprised to find a few windows still shining bright. At least a few employees were burning the midnight oil.

"Twenty-four hours a day, there's always somebody here," Miori humble-bragged, guessing at Rentaro's thoughts.

"Shiba Heavy Weapons takes up all the floors here?"

"Uh-huh."

"Boy, you must be raking it in."

He meant to chide her with that, but Miori just brought a kimono sleeve up to her mouth and gave him a graceful titter. "We do," she said. "Our weapons make us a lot of profit, and—sad to say—they'll probably continue to do so for a while to come. It's a dangerous world out there."

"It doesn't bug you at all?" he asked. "Making weapons meant for killing people, and stuff?"

"Well, we sell bulletproof gear and armored vehicles for dealing with that, too, so..."

"Making the problem, then selling the solution, huh?" Rentaro muttered. Or he would have, had he not quashed the sentiment right before it tried to escape his lips. He was hardly one to talk. He was armed at nearly all times, theoretically so he could engage Gastrea at a moment's notice, and he even had explosive charges installed within his body. Whether he resented Shiba Heavy Weapons or not, he was practically the culmination of their labor.

The car entered the parking lot, rolling up to what looked like a security checkpoint. The guard glared at first, suspicious of these late-night visitors, but when he saw Miori's smiling face emerge from beneath the tinted glass, things changed quickly. "Oh, pardon me, ma'am!" he said, standing at attention. "You can go on ahead."

As they pressed on to Shiba premises, Rentaro realized that his mouth had gone slightly agape. In front of the entrance, there was a team of security guards that—between their Shiba-labeled, full-body combat gear and the assault rifles in their hands—looked like they belonged to some special-forces team. Maybe a paramilitary force, even. And judging by the way they patrolled in tandem, Rentaro observed, they were clearly well-trained.

"Odd how the security's a lot tighter here than at your house."

Miori gave off a bewitching smile, as if Rentaro had just complimented her. "I told you, it's a dangerous world out there. If anything ever happens, they're trained to suppress Gastrea in place of the police or civsecs. It's all Shiba equipment from head to toe, too, so it makes for good advertising."

"Huh," Rentaro said as he steered the car past them. Now that he was closer, he could see that what he thought were bulletproof vests were actually state-of-the-art Shiba combat exoskeletons, protecting body joints while boosting overall muscular strength about 80 percent. They were among the best of their kind, posting astonishing anti–shock wave and anti-penetration results in testing.

Rentaro had seen them in a catalog once, then briskly closed it shut when he saw how many zeroes were in the prices. But as he heard it, being part of the Shiba Heavy Weapons family would pretty much grant him the keys to the vault when it came to access. It made him a tad jealous.

Miori gauged his response, her eyes slitted and curious.

"Y'know, Satomi dear, do you think you could beat those guys if you really felt like it?"

Rentaro silently shook his head. Being attacked by a squad of well-trained, heavily armed troopers like these... He wouldn't last long.

Now the car approached the entrance to the main building. Miori got out, sporting all the grace of an actress at the Oscars. Rentaro, similarly sporting his gloves and sunglasses, followed suit, as did Hotaru.

The lobby entrance was completely glass-lined, and the security guards inside quickened Rentaro's pulse. Miori may have agreed to help him, but that didn't mean everyone at Shiba from the mailroom on up was his friend now. The guard quizzically sized up Rentaro and his party, which made Rentaro's heart beat even faster.

"Good evening, Miori. What brings you here this late?"

"Oh, you know, this and that. Do y'know if anyone's left in the analysis lab down on the third basement floor?"

The man at the front desk took a moment to check his display-mounted glasses. "No," he replied, "they're all gone for the night."

"Okay, well, we'll be down there for just a sec. These are my friends. Thanks!"

With a delicate wave of her hand, she pressed on. Rentaro and Hotaru solemnly followed, feeling eyes on their backs as they boarded the elevator and pushed the B3 button. As the doors closed, Rentaro heaved a stress-relieving sigh and removed his disguise gear.

"You think they recognized me?"

"I dunno," Miori sneered playfully, "but I don't think sunglasses at night ever give off too friendly a vibe, you know?"

Hotaru looked up. "Your family doesn't say anything about you visiting the office late-night, Miori?"

"Ooh, you called me by my first name and everything," Miori sarcastically replied before putting her fist against her chest. "Nothing to worry about there, though. I get into all kinds of naughty stuff. One time, I came here at like two in the morning and took out blueprints for guns and stuff."

With a beep, the elevator opened. Ahead was total darkness. It was a bit humid, suggesting the central air was off. The echoing of their footsteps told Rentaro that the ceiling was pretty high.

"Anyway," Miori said as she ran a pass through a nearby magnetic reader, "welcome, my dear Satomi."

Suddenly, the room was flooded with bright light, forcing Rentaro to shield his eyes and squint. Lights activated one by one across the floor, and only when they were all on did Rentaro realize the sheer enormity of the place. It looked every bit like an experimental laboratory, complete with rooms walled by reinforced see-through glass. Beakers, flasks, and a motley array of other lab tools lined the visible desks. Rentaro recognized what the centrifuges looked like, at least, but there was no telling what the giant plastic box one row down was. A DNA sequencer, maybe?

Miori had shown Rentaro around her company's gun manufacturing facility once—a very factorylike atmosphere. This, on the other hand, looked clean, refined, and—for lack of a better term—like the *future*.

"Can I have the sample you need analyzed, please?"

"*You're* gonna do it? Can you do that?"

She responded by taking another fan out from her kimono, this one iron-ribbed. Spreading it wide, she batted it at herself proudly.

"Well, ask a silly question! There's no machine in this entire building I can't use."

Rentaro, honestly astonished, took the film case with the Gastrea tissue sample out of his pocket and tossed it to Miori.

"Thanks."

"You got it," Miori replied with an endearing wink before turning her back to them and padding away in her sandals. Watching her go, Rentaro whispered another *Thanks* to her in his mind.

6

"What?!"

The blanket flew off his body as he rose, causing some of the other detectives to give him questioning stares. Inspector Shigetoku Tadashima paid them no mind as he pressed his phone against his ear. On the other end of the line, he could hear Yoshikawa, one of his detectives, blabber into the phone, his obvious excitement causing his tongue to trip over itself.

"I said Miori Shiba, daughter of the president of Shiba Heavy Weapons, has gone missing. I was staking out the front gate, and the limousine she always uses came out the exit. I tailed it. It stopped in front of Magata High School, where she goes for class. So I waited for a while, but no Miori came out. I took a peek into the limo's interior, and that's when I realized someone pulled the wool over my eyes. Then I—"

Tadashima ended the call before his coworker could finish, grabbed his jacket from the desk corner it was slumped over, and leapt out of the station's nap room, putting his jacket on as he stormed down the hall.

It *had* to be Rentaro Satomi. But what was he doing, taking the president's daughter with him? Unless they knew why, searching the city would be fruitless...

"Hey, wait a minute, please!"

Turning toward the strained voice behind him, he found a square-shouldered female officer approaching him, standing tall as she inserted herself between Tadashima and the exit ahead.

"How long have you gone without any sleep, sir? You should really take a longer break first."

"The suspect's not gonna wait until I'm done napping!"

"You're going to wreck your health! You aren't that young anymore."

"If *this* is all it takes to wreck my health, I'm not cut out to be a detective, anyway!"

He tried to push off the officer, already taken aback by his threatening tone, when something occurred to him. He took a closer look at her face.

"Hey, Shiba Heavy Weapons helps the force out a lot, too, right?"

The inspector's sudden question further surprised the newcomer. "Y-yes," she managed to reply, rubbing her chin as she thought it over. "They supply us with weaponry; they take on some of the criminal-science work for us...ballistics analysis, blood testing, DNA... That's all part of their work—"

"That's *it*!"

"Huh?"

"Great. Good job, Officer! The Shiba Heavy Weapons HQ building. Get me as much backup as we got available. I'm going on ahead."

Tadashima provided as much appreciation as he could for the glassy-eyed officer, then spun in place and flew out of Magata Station.

Rentaro Satomi and his gang, for whatever reason, had their sights on a truck loaded with Gastrea. Whatever they picked up from that, they had to be analyzing it somewhere. Which made the theory that they were running around with some kind of concrete goal in mind seem even more plausible for him now.

Tadashima turned the key in his vehicle, then pushed down as hard as he could on the accelerator.

Test fluid flowed through a lab-room flask as Miori expertly operated the analysis machine. Watching off to the side, Rentaro realized his amateur knowledge gave him no clue how far along in the process she was. He didn't have much else to do, so he headed for the stairway, figuring he might as well gain an understanding of the building's setup while he was there.

Checking the position of the emergency exits, he opened the metal door and started climbing the dimly lit stairwell. The rhythmic tapping of his soles against the flat stone helped energize his thought process.

He had already been targeted once by Hummingbird. The hideout they took such great pains to keep safe was now discovered. The enemy, whoever it was, was damn talented at sniffing him out. For all he knew, their gnarled hands were circling themselves around his neck at this very minute—

This is stupid.

Shaking off his paranoid delusions, he examined the plate on the wall and realized he was on the first floor. He decided to turn around, not wanting to run into those security guards again—and just as he did, he stopped at what sounded like an explosion.

A gunshot. A sound familiar enough to understand immediately.

Cold metal hit his ear as he placed it against the emergency-exit door. Another gunshot from the other side. This time, he could tell it was a small-caliber, high-speed round. That pretty much IDed the culprit. An assault rifle.

The gunshots continued off and on, followed by the sound of glass shattering. Then the sounds of scuffling, interspersed with screaming. Then, complete silence.

His palms coated with sweat, Rentaro slowly, soundlessly, cracked open the door. The thick stench of blood through it made his body shiver. Summoning up his resolve, he opened it all the way—only to groan at what he saw.

"What the hell…?"

The first thing Rentaro could see was a security soldier slumped on the ground, as if taking a quick siesta. But some manner of bladed weapon had cut a deep gash in his neck, the initial spray from which was now exhibited in all its horrific glory on a nearby modern-art canvas.

The lobby's chairs and desks were upturned. There was evidence of corpses being dragged around, as well as spent casings and the like. That, and a wide selection of dead security, the number of which would've taken a conscious effort to count. Some had their necks snapped by force, their legs bent in unnatural directions. Others had one or more limbs amputated.

The lights had been knocked out on this floor, except for a night-light on a lone counter, creating a sort of spotlight effect on the front-desk attendant.

His back was turned to Rentaro. Looking closer, there was a puddle of dark liquid at his feet, as if he had just had an accident.

Rentaro sidled around, Beretta in hand, toward the chair. The man was staring straight up, his neck slashed from ear to ear. His wide-open eyes were frozen for all time in a gaze of terror.

He checked for a pulse. No dice.

"Good God…"

Something like twenty security guards, and they were annihilated?

Rentaro's throat was dry. He tried to swallow his nerves, trying to keep his head on straight. Then he heard another scream from afar, mixed in with rifle fire. Looking toward the front lawn spread out across the Shiba Heavy Weapons entrance, he saw a lone surviving guard swinging his rifle around, firing blindly. Shell shock, no doubt.

"Hey!"

The guard took notice, unfortunately.

"Eeeyaaahh!!" he shouted as he turned the gun on him. Rentaro ducked under the front desk and covered his ears.

He didn't have to wait long. The glass covering the entrance shattered, as did the lone light fixture still illuminating the lobby. The darkness grew thicker.

"Hold your fire! I'm friendly!"

He risked waving his hand above the desk. Nothing. Then he looked up. The shooter, finally coming to his senses, ran up to him.

"H-help! Help me!"

"What happened?"

The guard had both hands latched on to his headgear, clearly in pain.

"I don't know! I looked at my buddy and he was hanging in midair. His, his head was stabbed. There was blood spraying everywhere. And then I just… I have no idea."

"What the hell's that mean…?!" Rentaro shouted.

"Don't ask me, man! That's what I wanna know!"

Sensing that panic was about to set in again, Rentaro put both hands on the guard's shoulders to calm him. In his clutches, the guard explained that he found one of his coworkers run through with a knife *and* with a broken neck in a spot where nobody else was in sight—as if killed by an invisible man.

It was extremely hard for anyone sane to believe. If it weren't for the grisly scene laid out before them—the sheer scope of it—Rentaro would have doubted the guard's current mental state.

This was *that group* again. The one pursuing him. They had released their grim reaper yet another time.

Rentaro had already taken care of Hummingbird, the killer of Kenji Houbara. Which meant there were two left…

He already knew the sniper Dark Stalker, aka Yuga Mitsugi, had murdered Giichi Ebihara. This assassin still had something up his sleeve, he sensed—but was he the type who could break people's necks with his bare hands?

Meanwhile, the killer of Saya Takamura was still at large. Was *that* person the one behind this?

"I'm gonna get Miori out of this building. That's the rear entrance back there, right?"

The guard made a face like he just realized the existence of the rear gate for the first time. He made a break for it.

"Whoa! Wait a sec!"

"Get outta here!" the guard shouted behind his back as he ran. "I can't spend another minute in this hellhole!"

Then something Rentaro found hard to believe happened.

As he ran, from out of thin air, a large knife stabbed through the guard's exoskeleton and right out the other side. There was a sort of *shhkk* sound, and then his body was lifted off the ground.

"Ga...aaa...!"

Rentaro stood bolt upright as he witnessed the otherworldly spectacle. *What on...?*

There was nothing but utterly empty space where the knife had come from. It was like the weapon had leapt up and plunged itself into his chest on its own volition. Did a ghost stab him or something?

"You...monster...!"

The guard writhed violently in midair, kicking at his adversary. Then Rentaro spotted it: a sort of waving of the air, a bit like the noise seen in a poor digital TV signal. The air flickered, and he could see human-shaped visual garbage flicker in and out of sight.

He was *there*. Someone *had* stabbed him after all. A pretty *large* someone, at that.

Could this be—?

Rentaro could think of only one property of physics that could explain this unexplainable sight—and one type of equipment that could make it possible.

"Optical camo...?"

Whispering it to himself didn't make it any easier to believe.

The ability to bend the light around an object, making it melt into the background. The classic "invisible person," but something that still went beyond the framework of modern science.

And did this invisible giant lie in ambush there, waiting for his poor victim to run blindly for the rear exit? This was the man who destroyed all this military tech, the pride of Shiba Heavy Weapons?

The guard, still aloft, vomited a round of dark blood, then stopped moving. Tossing the body aside, the invisible man—Rentaro sensed—turned his eyes toward him. Murderous intent radiated from the space.

Rentaro's breathing grew short and shallow. It was too dangerous to stay there. Using the toe of his shoe, he kicked a rifle on the floor up into his hands, flipping the switch to full-auto mode and firing. It spat out an impressive amount of flash as it sprayed bullets across the wall of a nearby hallway with an ear-piercing roar.

But it was out of ammo in two seconds. *Time to run.*

Rentaro threw down the weapon and went back down the way he came, half running, half lunging for the stairwell. At the bottom, he tackled the B3 door open.

Hotaru and Miori, looking at a piece of paper, turned to him.

"Satomi, we've got the analysis results."

"The enemy's here," he panted. "It's *bad.*"

Hotaru narrowed her eyes. "Where?"

"I don't know. But we can't stay here." Rentaro turned. "Miori, that VR training space is still two floors down from here, right? I need to use it."

"A VR training space?"

"Yeah," he replied to Hotaru's doubtful query. "This, ah, enormous cube-shaped space that we use as a battle simulator. We'll take the guy on in there."

It was a curt explanation, but one good enough for Hotaru. She nodded. He turned toward Miori again.

"The enemy's after all three of us. You go to some other room and run the simulator for me. Shut off the door completely so no one can get in."

"All right. I just explained the results to Hotaru. She'll give you the story once we're clear."

"Got it."

Rentaro pushed the elevator button, and then set his hand on a gracefully hesitant Miori's shoulder.

"I really hope you don't have to die, Satomi dear," she said in reply.

"Already happened once, apparently. Don't really feel like having it happen again."

He nodded at her, conveying his resolve and thanks at the same time. The door closed.

"Let's go, Hotaru."

With new determination, Rentaro began to run. Taking three steps at a time as he tore downstairs, he checked the nameplate by the fifth underground floor's entrance and jumped inside.

Beyond the doorway was a locker room with two Shiba-branded assault rifles. Rentaro grabbed them both and tossed one to Hotaru. Next, he pushed open a nearby door that had a card reader mounted to one side.

Although he was expecting it, the brightness made him raise up his arm in self-defense.

It was a clear white space, so white that it was hard to tell the walls from the floor. It was completely empty, not a speck of dust at their feet. It was surreal, like nothing of this world—and, to someone experiencing it for the first time, a jaw-dropping experience.

Hotaru gingerly took a step forward. The result was enough to convince her the floor was really there, but stupefaction was still written all over her face. Rentaro beckoned her over.

As they walked across the vast cavern, the white began to twist and turn before them. Rentaro felt a sharp sense of dizziness for an instant, then the view around him changed 180 degrees.

It was now dark, humid, and musty. Rentaro could smell dust, and no light came in through the windows, which were framed by bare wood. The scent of rust and decomposing forest matter indicated this "building" had been abandoned for a while.

They were inside a dark, high-ceilinged space. Some kind of storage facility.

"Wh-what's this?" a wary Hotaru asked.

"The name of the stage is 'the warehouse,'" Rentaro replied as calmly as possible. "That's the cool part about VR battle training. You can change the entire combat environment at the push of a button."

Presumably this stage was Miori's decision.

"This is…virtual?" Hotaru asked as she curiously poked at a nearby storage crate. Beside her, Rentaro took a penlight out from his hip pocket and swung it around. Large piles of square crates sprung out from the darkness, carelessly layered in haphazard stacks or piles, all covered in a fine coating of dust.

The space seemed resentful of being awoken from its slumber; the only environmental lighting was slight and came from the opposite wall, a surprisingly long distance away. The chamber itself was about as large as a decent-size factory.

Rentaro placed his rifle on top of a nearby crate, deploying its bipod for stability as he aimed at the door they had arrived through. He peered into the dot sight as he gave Hotaru a quick rundown of how to operate the rifle.

"All right. So the enemy's gonna open this door and run through. He's using optical camo, so expect him to be invisible. Once it opens, start firing, whether you see anything or not."

"Gotcha."

Through the gunsight, Rentaro could see a pale red dot in the center of his view, jiggling to and fro in response to his pinpoint adjustments.

After a few moments, there was a faint clanging sound. The door was being pushed from the other side.

Rentaro's pulse raced. He sharpened the corners of his eyes, put his finger on the trigger, and pushed down enough to eliminate the play on it. The door opened enough to be slightly ajar.

"Hotaru!"

Full-auto fire ensued. The door was instantly pockmarked with holes, the blinding flash and concussive noise continuing on for what felt like eons. Eternity didn't last long, however, because the ammo was soon exhausted. A small moment of silence, and then a figure fell forward, onto the warehouse floor, the now unhinged door doing little to break his fall.

Rentaro gave a hand signal to his partner, took out his handgun, and approached. Gradually, he could see a silhouette via the glare behind him—a fully visible one. Either he'd turned off his optical camo or it was destroyed in the barrage.

Rentaro went up to the body, giving it a slight nudge with his foot. No response. Taking that as a cue, Rentaro crouched down and turned the body over. Then he froze.

"It's not the guy, Hotaru," Rentaro shouted behind him. "We've still got an active hostile!"

The man, presumably in his early thirties and dressed in nothing but a shirt and his boxers, was the security guard who lost his life just a moment ago. The enemy threw the corpse through the door to attract their fire.

*   *   *

"—I've been looking for you, 'New Humanity.' My name is Swordtail."

The voice came from behind.

Rentaro turned around just in time to see a knife, floating in the air, descending rapidly upon him.

"Shi—"

Rentaro immediately pictured it—the knife piercing deep into his chest cavity and skewering his heart. But before it became reality, there was a gunshot. It *ting*ed against the knife, sending it across the floor.

Support fire from Hotaru. Rentaro crouched down as she continued the salvo without any rest, firing blindly with both hands.

The bullets carved the warehouse's walls, but they were just a moment too late. The enemy's ghostly form had vanished again.

Hotaru grabbed on to Rentaro. Before he could ask why, he felt another powerful acceleration, as if being blown away by an explosion. The girl, reasoning it was too dangerous to remain there, had leapt upward.

"How the hell're we gonna beat *that*?!"

"I'm trying to think of something, all right?!"

The two landed in the central area of the warehouse, Rentaro on Hotaru's back.

"You murdered Saya Takamura, didn't you?!" he shouted into the unfathomable darkness.

"Hohh," a voice echoed across the expansive warehouse space, its position impossible to detect. "You've dug yourself in that deep and you're still breathing, huh? No wonder the group's running itself ragged trying to find you."

As he spoke, Rentaro's mind raced for a potential solution. His enemy was invisible, and yet his knife wasn't. His invisibility was the result of some kind of cloak or vest, perhaps, but whenever he attacked, maybe that meant his weapon had to be exposed for that one moment before the strike.

And it wasn't like the camo could nullify his footsteps or sense of presence. If the enemy didn't have any close-quarters weaponry besides that knife, Rentaro could always use his five senses to figure out where he was. If there was a handgun or something on his person, though, that complicated things.

But who is this Swordtail guy, anyway...?

"Lemme guess what you're thinking right now. It's something like *How's he able to camouflage his entire body?* Right?"

Rentaro's mouth snapped shut.

"You know how Dark Stalker has a copy of Sumire Muroto's 21-Form Varanium Artificial Eye. Hummingbird had an upgraded clone of Ain Rand's Shenfield tech. Meanwhile, I'm installed with something called the 'Marriott injection,' something originally meant for mechanized infantry. My nanomaterial-infused skin can bend the light around it at will. It's the most powerful skill a robot soldier can have, and Arthur Zanuck made it practical for real-life use."

"Wha—?!"

Arthur Zanuck... He'd heard that name before. One of the so-called Four Sages alongside Sumire. So Swordtail was another one of their skill mimickers... But what did that mean? Whoever was behind the New World Creation Project, what were they trying to—?

Amid the mazelike piles of metal containers strewn all over the place, Rentaro turned his attention left and right, guard ever on the ready. Nobody seemed to be nearby. The sound drained itself from the shabby warehouse, and he felt completely alone. Every cell of his skin was attuned like radar, ready to pick up so much as a pin dropping.

Suddenly, the hairs on the back of his neck stood up.

"Nice try."

The human hand that came out of the darkness set a gun to rest comfortably against Rentaro's temple.

Rentaro reacted. Just before the trigger was pulled, he brushed the gun away and darted his head to the side. There was a loud *crack* from the gun, then a rush of heat as the bullet grazed his temple.

Rentaro dropped to the floor, executed a forward roll, then got right back on his feet. He drew his gun on the enemy, but he was already gone.

"Don't you know about me? You would if you'd done your research."

A half-pitying, half-chiding voice sounded off, this time in point-blank range of his ears. Rentaro was taken by surprise—it was exactly like before, except this time the point of the gun was right at his back.

"You can try as many times as you want. But you can't win."

But there, faster than the naked eye could see, Hotaru plowed in.

"*Nrh!*"

Turning around, Rentaro found that Hotaru had deftly made her way to the giant man's hand, using her entire body to squeeze the gun out of it. The optical camo flickered out—perhaps not as effective when grappling with a foe like this—revealing an eerily large man in a coat. Rentaro could hear his muscles creaking, screaming for help, all the way from his vantage point.

"God damn—"

But their enemy was still up to the task. His muscles grated one another as he jerked his wrist back, not caring if he dislocated it or not, and shook Hotaru off. Hotaru slammed against the ground back-first. Swordtail drew his gun on her.

By the time Rentaro thought *Oh crap*, his body was already running, all but slamming into her. As he did, two gunshots overlapped each other. Pain wrenched his back. He gritted his teeth.

Hotaru, held down on the ground, opened her eyes wide in surprise, her eyes shaking. "Rentaro…! What are you—?"

The blood dripping out the back of his school uniform fell upon Hotaru's face. She shook it off in disbelief and screamed.

"You're so *stupid*! I can regenerate myself at will! You didn't have to—"

"—Shut up!"

Hotaru instantly fell silent.

"I *really* don't like that attitude of yours."

"Stop it! You're gonna die!"

Swordtail fired another flurry of bullets. They all struck home on his back.

"Gaaaaaahh!!"

Hotaru shook her head back and forth again. "Stop! Please, just stop!" she barely managed to whisper, tears forming in the corners of her eyes.

"At least let me protect my partner *this* time!"

"It's over, kid," came a voice from behind. There was no way to instantly react to it. The end was near. Rentaro's body tightened, anticipating the heat from the bullets coming the next instant.

Then he was tossed aside without warning.

Gunshots. Blood sprayed from Hotaru's left breast, right on the heart. For a moment, Rentaro didn't realize what had happened.

But Hotaru was dead. The moment he realized it, rage seared him from head to toe.

"You piece of—"

He couldn't afford to have the enemy go invisible again. He got up, spewing blood, and with all his might, planted his feet on the ground and calmed himself. A cartridge spat itself out of his leg, spinning, and propelled his foot upward.

Tendo Martial Arts Second Style, Number 14—

"Inzen Genmeika!"

The midlevel kick, launched from a low, near-crouching position, found its mark. It hit cleanly on the chest area of the giant, a look of shock burned onto his face.

The force seemed to blow the air in all directions, the propulsion from Rentaro's leg sending the man flying like so many dead leaves in autumn. He collided with a stack of crates in the center of the room, kicking up plumes of dust as the collapsing pile tumbled over his body.

"Gnh!"

Rentaro's response was to vomit a thick splatter of blood across the floor. Firing a cartridge with open wounds on his body succeeded in ravaging all his injuries. But he could still move. And if his Tendo Martial Arts skills—further powered up by the jet turbine–like cartridges in his leg—found their target, it would be the same as being struck by a semitruck at full speed. In fact, it was a miracle his adversary's limbs didn't get blown off.

As he smelled something pungent among the dust, Rentaro used his free hand to cover his mouth so he didn't breathe it in. A moment later, he spotted Swordtail's brown coat. He was lying facedown, surrounded by a carpet of wood splinters, and his coat was the only part visible.

Rentaro went up to his enemy's feet and, without hesitation, pulled the trigger on his Beretta twice. If the man was playing possum, well, now he wasn't.

The bullets shredded the coat, sending fabric fibers flying, but there was no blood.

Something was off. Rentaro nudged at the coat with his fingertips, then decided to simply rip it off.

Before he could even consciously acknowledge surprise, his body had already planted itself against a nearby crate. Gingerly daring another look at the coat, he saw a pile of vaguely body-shaped splinters under it, and nothing else. No body.

Rentaro felt something to his left. He pulled his chin back, his body falling in reverse, and a fist the size of a boulder thundered past his head. He was now out of position, and he had no way of evading the foe as he advanced upon him at astounding speed. He, and his combat boot.

"*Gah!*"

"That wasn't a bad idea," a monotonous voice said from across the dark warehouse. By the time Rentaro's bleary vision focused itself again, he realized Swordtail was standing no more than a meter away from him.

The man was damaged. The cuffs of his pants were frayed, and he was bleeding. Breathing, for him, required heaving his shoulders up and down. Without the coat, he could see that the man, his hulking body shaped something like an inverted triangle, was wearing a black tank top.

"But you just *had* to go around thinking I was on the same level as somebody like Hummingbird."

Swordtail aimed his handgun at Rentaro's head. A bottomless abyss awaited within it.

"You lose."

"And that arrogance just made *you* lose."

No one was more surprised than Swordtail to see a figure perched on top of him, as if he was giving her a piggyback ride.

"You... Why are you...?!"

Hotaru had both feet laced around the bucking Swordtail's head, using her free hands to draw her twin pistols from behind her back.

"I hope you taste even a tenth of the suffering Kihachi did."

The next moment, a continual cycle of explosions and muzzle flashes swarmed the area. Fresh, warm blood fell upon Rentaro's face.

"Aaaahhhhh!"

With a beastlike roar as he desperately tried to peel Hotaru off, Swordtail found himself the target of a merciless pair of .45-caliber handguns as they thudded their payloads into him at point-blank range.

The otherworldly sight didn't last long. Soon the slide stops popped up on both weapons, indicating they had exhausted their ammo. Hotaru leapt out of the way.

"*Ngh*...ahh...!"

Swordtail fell to his knees, then face-first onto the ground with a mighty, earth-shaking *foom*.

"Rentaro!" Hotaru shouted as she all but threw herself at him, embracing his head. He couldn't feel the sensation, which wasn't exactly encouraging, but Rentaro weakly nodded nonetheless. The chill from the blood loss was making his eyes heavy. Hotaru shook him as hard as she could.

"We need to get out of here and get you treated!"

He got back on his feet, Hotaru lending him a shoulder, and forced his knees to not buckle. He was cold. He'd lost too much blood; he felt like he'd freeze to death before anything else.

Rentaro took a side glance at Swordtail—only to have the sight shoot a jolt of reenergizing surprise into him.

The huge man was gone without a trace. In his place were blood-stains, with a trail of droplets following out of the room.

"Hotaru... He ran on us..."

"How?! How could he have moved after that?"

"I don't know...but looks like he did."

Anyone involved in either the New Humanity or the New World Creation Projects were people with strength beyond all reason. Applying Varanium to human bones and organs had the terrifying power to turn mortal wounds into not-so-mortal ones.

"We gotta go after him... We can't let him leave with the info we have."

Swordtail, also known as Jugo Katake, slammed a fist against the wall as he entered the shower room, all but ripping the curtain off the pole as he stormed into a booth. He used the knob to set the temperature to 36 degrees Celsius—suitable for washing blood spatter off his body—and immersed his head in the lukewarm water.

It couldn't be. It couldn't. Not this, Jugo whispered to himself as he struggled to take hold over his consciousness.

His powerful carbon-nanotube muscles, combined with a spinal column made of self-repairing Varanium alloy, had stopped all the bullets. His blood vessels had constricted themselves to prevent excessive blood loss. The organic transistors implanted in his body had monitored all medical statistics relevant to keeping him alive, making adjustments as necessary.

And yet the flurry of handgun fire Jugo took at point-blank range wasn't anything he could ignore. Especially given how physical brawn was such a key part of his battle strategy.

The blood now washed off his body, he checked to make sure his optical camo still worked as usual, then flew out of the shower and began his escape. On the elevator he went, jumping over the dead security guards still decorating the first-floor lobby, and soon he was outside, greeted by the murky, humid night air.

He couldn't shake the frustration that bubbled up. He was supposed to be the brightest star of the New World Creation Project. So how did an obsolete pre-war model leave him in the dust like that?

What part of me could possibly *be inferior to him?*

"Well, *someone* just got put through the wringer."

"Who—?"

He was in the central courtyard of the Shiba Heavy Weapons building when a figure emerged from under one of the poplar trees that dotted the well-kept lawn. Jugo winced in disbelief once the moonlight fully exposed the boy.

"Dark Stalker?!"

He wanted to know what the kid was doing there, but he resisted the urge to ask. This was too good an opportunity to let pass.

"Perfect. Report to Hitsuma through Nest for me. I landed a lethal blow on Hotaru Kouro, but she came back to life. Whatever her Gastrea element is, it gives her an incredible amount of vitality."

"Yeah? Thanks for the report."

The carefree, inattentive tone of voice made Jugo wonder if he even realized how vital this was. He swung an arm out, frustrated.

"What're you doing?! The enemy's coming! Let me go!"

"Afraid I can't agree to that."

"What?"

"I know it's kind of a summary judgment, but I need to execute you right here. You screw up, you die."

For a moment, Jugo stared blankly, unsure what Dark Stalker had just said.

"What kind of joke is that?"

"Sorry, but it's not any kind of joke at all. You lost, and as a result, the group told me they don't want anything to do with you."

"I haven't lost at all yet!"

"You're the only one who thinks that, you know."

Hold on... Is he really going to...?

"W-wait a minute. Just give me another chance."

"Don't need to." Yuga brushed his hair back, the spite practically radiating from his face. "Is it that hard to believe? That you might wind up being the executed instead of the executioner sometime?"

There was no way he could. Jugo had given everything to the group. Why would they treat him like this? "...And you think I'm just gonna let myself get killed?" he demanded.

Yuga shrugged. "Well, that's what I'm here for, anyway."

Swordtail lowered his body into a battle stance. "That's insane! *You're* the one who deserves to die. Go ahead. Ask Mr. Hitsuma anytime you want. The group isn't gonna just dump me like that!"

The pain from before was gone now. All the adrenaline his body generated had pushed his ability to sense discomfort deep into his subconscious. He checked his legs, and other parts, too. His organs and respiratory system were damaged, but less than half of Jugo's body was organic, anyway. Everything else was the fruit of modern bioelectronics, a far cry from anything in nature's creation.

He lowered his breathing—and with it, his body temperature. Glaring into his adversary's eyes, he took off, activating his optical camo to make his body a mirage in the wind.

He had heard about Yuga's cybernetic eyes. But this was exactly the kind of match he wanted—a fighter given a skill so advanced that he couldn't help but be bound by it in his tactics.

Jugo made no sound as he sidled around his foe, attempting to get closer. Dark Stalker was still looking at Jugo's position from a moment ago; taking out his auxiliary knife, Jugo approached from the right-hand side like a predator stalking its prey—and then slashed forward at full speed. To someone like him, a veteran of undercover assassination, this was his killer move. By the time his target realized he was under attack, his head would already have been separated from his torso.

Immediately afterward, Dark Stalker's head would arc through the air. He could picture it already.

But what he didn't anticipate was his foe's right hand flying up, his head still pointed forward.

He saw the hand brush against the blade of his knife. Then he heard the crunch of crumpled steel. Jugo's vision shook, as if he was being electrocuted, and his optical camo peeled right off.

He leapt back reflexively, struggling to regain equilibrium. When he did, Jugo saw his stainless-steel knife in his hand, crushed from the tip of the blade to the handle.

Jugo shuddered as the bladeless handle fell from his hands, unable to believe the sight.

"That's…crazy…!"

"What is? The fact that you had no idea what you were getting into when you attacked me? Or the fact that lame optical camo of yours was neutralized at the single wave of a hand?"

Dark Stalker smirked and shrugged his shoulders at his adversary, now shocked into submission. "I like that Marriott injection and all the other stuff you use for that invisibility trick of yours," he said, arms open wide, "but none of that mattered after I got you in my sight. The processors in both of my eyes spotted the way you flexed your muscles and calculated your strategic approach—even the position you'd show up at. It's almost like they predict the future for me. All I have to do is keep myself from yawning while you telegraph your punches from a mile away."

"But… But how did you pulverize my knife just by touching it?!" Jugo yelled, looking down at the cracked, shattered pieces of metal on the ground. Come to think of it, he *did* hear about Dark Stalker being equipped with some kind of experimental armament. "S-some kind of ultrasonic wave device?"

As Jugo finished shouting the question, Yuga was upon him, a lethal palm placed upon his heart.

"Well done. I think you should taste it for yourself, though. Isn't modern technology amazing? It takes the concepts of physical strength, the idealism of martial arts, and turns it all on its head."

Then, without any time to curse his regrets, Jugo experienced the vibrating waves from Yuga's death-dealing palm destroy the very connections between his skin and muscle cells.

"This is my second power. It's called Vairo-orchestration."

The pain was intense for Jugo—like his organs were being put through a blender. His heart was quickly pulverized, no time provided to even conceptualize any last words as his consciousness faded into darkness.

There was a *splurt*, something no simple palm strike could ever produce, as Swordtail coughed up enough blood to form a puddle around his feet. He tottered dangerously, eyes staring in disbelief at Rentaro—before he fell like a tree to the ground. There was no getting back up this time.

Rentaro had made his way out of the Shiba Heavy Weapons building just in time to witness a sight he never expected—two New World Creation Project veterans attempting to kill each other. He couldn't imagine what brought this chain of events about, but either way, Swordtail had just fallen with a single hit.

Yuga's victory couldn't have been more complete. It was barely even a match. A scar in the shape of his hand remained on Swordtail's chest as the man lay dead on his back. The strike must've had the effect of necrotizing the local tissue. Even the palm's prints were clearly discernible.

It was the same skill that Rentaro had luckily escaped at the Plaza Hotel. If there was an ace up Yuga's sleeve, that had to be it. Rentaro felt a cold twinge, like someone had slipped an ice cube down the back of his shirt. He steeled himself, fists balled up tight, and began to walk up to Yuga. They were face-to-face again, not ten meters away from each other in the Shiba courtyard.

"Yuga...Mitsugi..." came the resentful, whispered words from Rentaro's mouth. Ever since they'd first met—ever since Mitsugi had shot him out of the skies above the hotel—he could never forget that name. Nor could he forget the fact that both were doomed to fight each other again someday.

"We finally meet," came the joyful reply as Yuga put his arms out wide in a gesture of welcome. "Not quite when I was expecting it, though. I didn't think Swordtail would do *that* bad of a number on you."

"This doesn't hurt at all."

Rentaro was wobbly, his vision bleary at best. But at least the blood coming out of his mouth was close enough to the color of his uniform that it didn't stand out too much.

Yuga's lips loosened into a piteous smile. "Well, if you've gotten to see Swordtail in battle for yourself, I guess you realize who you're dealing with in New World now, don't you?"

"The New World Creation Project is a second-generation team of mechanized soldiers, in the style of the New Humanity Creation Project program," Rentaro stated. "The eyes you use to fight with were copied from plans developed by Dr. Sumire Muroto, one of the Four Sages. Hummingbird's thought-activation interface was borrowed from research conducted by Ain Rand. Swordtail's skills were copied from Arthur Zanuck. Dr. Muroto told me that developing artificial eyes or limbs required knowledge across so many different fields that most researchers can't even understand the basic concepts that drive them. And if you think about it, it must take one hell of a genius to not only copy that stuff, but to upgrade it, too. In fact, I can think of only one person."

Yuga arched his eyebrows in curiosity.

"Let's hear it."

Rentaro looked down at Yuga, jaw still jutted forward.

"The person beating the war drum for your dirty project is the last of the Four Sages—Albrecht Grünewald."

Yuga, in apparent agreement, lifted his hands high into the air. "Well done! And the name of our group is the Five Wings Syndicate! Happy to make your acquaintance!"

"The Five Wings...?"

"Take a look at this."

Yuga rolled up the right sleeve of his school uniform, showing off his triceps. What Rentaro saw tattooed there made him gasp.

"The pentagram...and the wings..."

He had seen it several times by then, but Yuga's star mark had four ornately designed wings drawn around it. Two wings, however, appeared to have been erased in some fashion. Apparently doing so wasn't easy, since they had been crudely scratched out, like a kinder-gartener's scribble-scrabble with a crayon over a coloring-book page.

Yuga smiled as Rentaro looked on. "Yeah, I kinda had two wings plucked off me. Now I can't fly anymore. I fell back to earth."

"...I've seen that in a few places now. All on things associated with the Five Wings Syndicate, I guess. Is the number of wings some kind of ranking system?"

"Well, if you know that much, I can cut right to the chase, I guess. You're right. Five wings indicate one of the group's core leaders. It goes down to four, three, and two wings after that. One wing marks you as either a follower or a slave—or maybe house pet, I guess. If you feel like frisking Swordtail's body over there, there's probably a two-wing mark on him somewhere."

Rentaro could feel the fog lift from his mind little by little. He decided to prod their discussion just a bit further along.

"When I visited Dr. Ayame Surumi's apartment, I got a call from someone disguising his voice and warning me about Hummingbird. That was you, right?"

A gust of wind flew around them, lifting Rentaro's, Yuga's, and a watching Hotaru's hair up. There was a rustle as the surrounding trees swayed gently.

"That wasn't me, no."

"The hell it wasn't. Why? Why did you take action to help me?"

Yuga responded with silence for a few moments before sighing, apparently opting to give up the charade.

"Satomi, has the beauty of the world around you ever made you want to cry?"

"What?"

"I was born blind in both eyes."

Rentaro was thrown by this. He was starting to lose track of the subject.

"My mother fell ill while she was pregnant with me, and that's kind of what happened. One hundred percent blind. It never particularly bothered me at the time. You can't miss what you never had in the first place, and stuff. But you know how cruel other kids can be. By the time I made it to elementary school, they picked on me all the time. It really made me angry. But it was Professor Grünewald who saved me, along with his second-generation mechanized-soldier plan. That was already under development in secret by the time I showed up. And as you've probably noticed, my '21-Form' allows me to see even when I don't have it activated, unlike your eye."

Yuga shook his head a little, then turned directly toward Rentaro. The color of his eyes was gone, replaced with a dangerous-looking glare that felt sharp enough to cut with.

"Once I joined their ranks, the beauty of a springtime day honestly made me cry. So did the summer sun, beating down on my eyes. The colors of autumn did it to me all over again, and so did the whiteness of winter. I felt like I couldn't possibly ask for anything else, and that I needed to give the Professor everything that I possibly could in return. That's why I built myself up. I mean, I was absorbed heart and soul in the training they gave me. That's what earned me four wings in the end. I was the Professor's prodigal son. He gave me VIP treatment. And then…"

All the tension Yuga had built up fell off a self-chiding cliff with the *and then*.

"I messed it up *just once*, and that cost me two wings. The Professor branded me a failure, and now I'm up to my neck in this dirty assassin business. You wanted to know why I'd do anything to help you, yeah? Don't make me laugh. I didn't do that for *your* sake or anything. I just couldn't stand the concept of some tin soldier like Hummingbird or Swordtail doing you in. That's all."

He steeled his resentful eyes at Rentaro, denying him the chance to offer any semblance of compassion.

"The Professor promised me that if I beat you, he'd give me my wings back. Once I do, I can go back to serving him again."

Rentaro had never met Grünewald. But if he was the type of academic to personally brand Yuga a failure, and then dangle the chance of rehabilitation in front of him if he killed Rentaro…then he hadn't seen much to respect about the man yet. Ain Rand, Tina's mentor, was the same way. Something told him the three other Sages didn't care much about virtue or common decency, unlike Sumire.

"And you think Grünewald's justified in this? In forcing you to commit first-degree murder?"

"It's not a matter of whether the Professor's justified or not. All that matters is whether I believe in him or not."

Yuga turned his back then, only to shoot him a sidelong glance.

"I will await you at the site of the final battle. We can conclude it there."

With that, without taking another look back, Yuga left the scene. Soon, he was gone from Shiba Heavy Weapons property. Rentaro stared intently at him the whole time, convinced he'd turn around at any moment. But after a while, when he'd disappeared and hadn't returned, Rentaro let out a deep sigh.

In the process, he realized his vision was lurching sideways a little. Hotaru stopped him before it went fully vertical, but the damage was done. *Yuga must have realized*, Rentaro thought ruefully, *the state of total exhaustion I'm in.*

"We better head back to the hideout, Rentaro."

From some indistinct corner of the city, the familiar sound of sirens blared. It sounded like it was headed straight for them.

Hotaru scowled. "That's a lot of 'em, judging by the sound."

"Ah, the Knights of the Round Table. Just a *little* too late, once again."

Hotaru flashed him a look. "If you got enough energy to spout stupid crap like that, you'll be okay if I'm a little rough getting us out, right?"

"A little rough?"

Hotaru turned her head almost straight up. Rentaro followed her eyes. They were pointed at the roof of the main building.

"They'll track us down if we keep running. I wanna jump away from there."

The door opened with a crisp electronic beep. Rentaro braced a shaky arm against the elevator wall as he exited, Hotaru propping him up. They were greeted by a howl and a gust of surging wind. Turning his head, he could see the red, yellow, and blue neon flash down below, just past the helipad. The lights from the swarm of police cars at the bottom. Another familiar sight.

The hand around Rentaro's shoulder was warm. Worth his trust. Far more than usual, at least.

"Let's go. Grab on to me."

He tried to thank her. He couldn't quite manage it, his pallid, zombie-like lips and semifrozen skin no longer listening to his instructions.

But—

"Freeze! Do anything funny, and I'll shoot!"

Rentaro and Hotaru stopped at the sound of a handgun's cylinder rotating behind them.

"Lemme see your hands. Walk slowly back toward my voice. Slowly!"

Rentaro raised his hands, not wanting to rile the gunman, and turned around. There he saw a police detective, a stern look on his face as he readied his pistol in both hands.

"Inspector Tadashima…"

Hotaru lowered her stance, readying for battle. Rentaro raised a hand to stop her, then took a step forward.

The humid night wind blew fiercely across the space between Rentaro and Shigetoku Tadashima, making their clothes flap violently in the air.

"Are you people half-bird or something? Every damn time I see you, you're on the roof of some high-rise. You gotta be nuts."

Rentaro tried moving his jaw. It seemed to work well enough to speak.

"Let us go, Inspector."

"No! I'm here in the name of the law. And it's my duty to uphold it. The law is the only beacon of order this world has. We'd be in total darkness without it. What would we call a world without order? It wouldn't be a civilization. It'd be chaos."

"So you're gonna just neglect justice?"

"Oh, you think *you're* in the right here? Look, what's going on behind the scenes with you? What do you know?"

"I told you a hundred times in the interrogation room."

"Oh, so all the delusional bullshit you gave me in *extreme* detail in your testimony is true? Don't give me that crap!"

"The group I'm fighting is spreading chaos. They're destroying that order you were talking about. And now you're helping it grow. Saying 'I didn't know' isn't gonna help you. It's *your* fault you're so clueless. I'm outta here."

"You think I'm gonna say you can go?"

"Atsuro Hitsuma's an enemy spy. He's infiltrated the police department."

"He is *not*!" Tadashima shook his head in obvious mental distress and turned away. "That's...not true...!"

"Okay. Shoot me, then."

Hotaru shot Rentaro a surprised look. "Rentaro, wait a...!"

"Don't move, Hotaru. I want to handle things properly with this guy."

Tadashima turned back, and Rentaro addressed him:

"If you think you're right, then shoot me. If you arrest me, you know they'll find me guilty. I might die in prison, for all I know. That's how far the enemy's sunk its teeth in you."

"Don't be stupid. We're the police. We're duty-bound to protect the accused."

"That won't help," Rentaro insisted. "That's how this enemy works."

Tadashima's lips pursed.

"So I'm guessing by your reaction that you know Atsuro Hitsuma, huh? If you've been with him before, did you notice anything weird about him?"

The detective froze. The proverbial cat had gotten his tongue. He tried to conceal his expression, but the effort shamed him.

"Right. So you *have* noticed something, but he's your boss, so you have to suck up to him instead?"

Tadashima was silent.

Rentaro closed his eyes and shook his head. "So shoot me. You'll get a certificate of honor out of it, won't you?"

"I—I..."

Tadashima's body began to shake, his index finger wrapped around the gun apparently frozen in place. His face was covered in greasy sweat.

"If you ain't shooting, we're leaving."

Rentaro motioned an order at Hotaru, hung on to her shoulder, then fell forward.

"Whoa! Hey!"

Tadashima hurriedly peered down the side of the roof. But the boy in black had already melted into the night, gone without a trace.

"Argh!!"

Driven by anger bubbling over, Tadashima pointed his gun to the sky and fired three times. The three shots echoed through the air, catching rides on the gusting wind. They did nothing to quell the anger aimed at himself. He tossed the gun to the side, then fell to his knees, not caring about the pain as he batted a fist against the roof several times.

"Why?! Why couldn't I shoot him?!"

He *had* to shoot him. He had to prove that the law, such as it was, supported him. He had to prove he was Shigetoku Tadashima, and that the brunt of his will could only be expressed by killing the hated criminal that reared its ugly head before him.

But he failed.

Something in him doubted whether Rentaro was a criminal. The odd obsession with secrecy Hitsuma brought into the investigation had made him arch his eyebrows one too many times.

That meant defeat. The law, the concept he worshiped to the point of believing there was never any way to cheat one's way out of it, had lost. Shigetoku Tadashima's "law" had been brought to its knees by the immature, childish "justice" that civsec just *had* to bring into the picture.

"Inspector! What are you doing up here?!"

He turned around to find Yoshikawa, white as a sheet, running up to him. He must have heard the gunshots. Tadashima quickly felt his thoughts start to cool down. Wiping the dust from his pants, he stood up and walked past his underling.

"I'm leaving this investigation for a little bit. I found something that I have to look into. Superintendent Hitsuma's probably gonna be here in a bit. Take your orders from him."

"I-Inspector? Inspector, what's going on? Inspector!"

He could feel the voice pulling at him from behind. But Tadashima ducked his head down low, never turning around, and left the scene.

He had to do it. He had to resolve these doubts in his mind. He had finally realized that he was no longer able to perform the basic duties of a police officer.

BLACK BULLET 6 CHAPTER 04

THE STARLESS NIGHT

He was in a dream.

There stood the Happy Building, soaked in the colors of twilight. Up the stairs he went, going through the door with the TENDO CIVIL SECURITY AGENCY plate on it. Enju's clothes were strewn all over the sofa, the sink on the other side of the curtain filled with dirty dishes.

The visitor sofa was always Tina's favorite. Her nocturnal schedule meant she slept there a lot, balled up like a cat. He peered over at the sofa, but there was no trace of her—just a somewhat worn-down pillow, suggesting it held her weight not long ago. There was a just barely started workbook of math drills on the nearby desk, along with a small pile of eraser shavings.

There was the sound of running water. Lifting the curtain to the cooking area, he found the sink was full of water from the neglected tap. It was already dampening Rentaro's socks.

It seemed so lived in, but nobody was there. Like the *Mary Celeste* of maritime lore. But Rentaro, for some reason, knew that.

They were gone. Kisara was gone. Enju and Tina were dead. Killed. Those days would never return. This office was an empty shell, as though someone had shot footage of the Tendo Civil Security Agency in happier days, spliced the beginning and end together, and put it on permanent loop. It was just a video image supported by his memories, and now someone had edited the entire cast of characters out.

It was indescribably sad. Besieged by regret, Rentaro fell to his knees on the spot, grasping his head and wailing his laments. A groan like a frog run over by a car emanated from his throat. *It's all my fault. Because I couldn't save any of them.*

Suddenly, he heard someone calling his name. A girl. She was pleading for him. He shook his head and searched for the voice. Where did it come from? Where was he hearing it from? It was neither Kisara's, nor Tina's, nor Enju's voice.

Right. That voice was—

The string of his dream was cut off, his consciousness gradually rising from the mud. His back was resting against something tough and unyielding, his body heavy. Sweat covered his clothing, and he was intensely thirsty.

But the voice was still calling him. With great effort, Rentaro blinked a few times and opened his eyes.

"What…? Shut up, man…"

The blurry world began to form images in his mind. Jolting his body into action, he realized it was Hotaru calling him. Her lips were pulled sharply back, her eyes red. A shock coursed across him.

"If you're alive, at least answer me!"

"Where am I…?"

Hotaru wiped her eyes with a sleeve. "The sculpture studio. Our hideout."

He finally recognized the familiar sight of the ceiling above him. Turning his head, Rentaro felt a jag of pain. *Oh, right. I took a bunch of bullets to the back.*

Nursing his neck, he looked down at his own body. His coat and shirt were off, and he was bandaged from below his armpits down to his stomach. It made him look like an enforcer from some yakuza flick.

He was, at least, alive.

Hotaru was back to her usual self to some extent, it seemed. She snorted at him, chin thrust haughtily into the air.

"I extracted the bullets. I think I got all of them, but no guarantees," she said.

It was then that multiple blobs of metal, a pair of tweezers, and a pile of bloody cotton strips next to him entered Rentaro's line of view.

"I'm impressed you could do that," he muttered.

"I had to do it on myself once."

That attracted his attention. He turned to her. "You've been shot that many times?"

"Yeah. Something wrong with that?"

"Nothing *wrong*, but…" He thought a bit about how far to pursue this, but before he could decide, he noticed the puffy bags around Hotaru's eyes.

"Have you been sleeping at all?"

Hotaru covered her eyes with her hands, apparently ashamed of the rings on her face. Then she suddenly turned defiant, puffing out her chest.

"No, all right? I couldn't, thanks to a certain idiot I got my ass teamed with. You better make up for this."

Rentaro snickered. It was just such an innocent display.

"Look… Um, why do you ask?" Hotaru shifted again. Now her voice was small, almost nonexistent. "You got hurt so bad, trying to cover me…Why do you have to do all these stupid things? I told you, I wanted to keep this strictly business. I use you; you use me. If you die, I don't take a look back. If the opposite happens, leave me on the sidewalk."

"Yeah, I remember," Rentaro lightly replied, trying to keep the subject from getting too heavy. Hotaru drooped her head and peevishly turned her back to him.

"You are *so* stupid."

A weird silence commenced. Neither were talking—and yet, the silence wasn't altogether uncomfortable, either. Rentaro didn't mind it, at least. But they couldn't afford to keep this going forever. They still had a mountain of issues to think about.

He gestured outside with a hand.

"It's pretty hot in here. Wanna go out for a bit?"

The moon was out.

A river flowed not far from the abandoned sculpture studio, swollen with the rain that fell from morning to late afternoon. The sound of the dark water bustling by them brought a refreshing coolness to their ears.

Rentaro and Hotaru were walking side by side along the embankment. Despite the late hour, they were still passed by the occasional old man walking his dog, or the would-be weekend warrior panting from a jog.

They had been walking downstream for a little while by the time Hotaru flashed Rentaro an exasperated look.

"Look, aren't you in pain at all? 'Cause you're sure impressing me. I guess your New Humanity Creation Project surgery lets you control your pain, huh?"

"Yeah, more or less," Rentaro lied. Pain seemed to ooze out of every pore in his body. To be honest, Hotaru would probably have to serve as his caretaker for a while to come. That wasn't something he could bargain with her about yet.

He could still remember the dream he had, albeit vaguely. He was on his knees, wailing in an empty Tendo Civil Security Agency bereft of Kisara, Tina, or Enju. That couldn't be *just* a dream. It was a very real problem, one that would be reality if he couldn't rescue any of them. And his brain was presenting that very likely scenario to him in dream form.

Which meant, by then, that they couldn't afford to waste another moment.

"Here, Rentaro."

Hotaru took something out of a breast pocket. Rentaro thought it was a fallen leaf or something at first, until he realized that it was in fact a rather oddly shaped key. The handle was made to look like a leaf from a maple tree, right down to special chemicals used to simulate the corrosion of the fall colors. It was an intricate piece of art.

"What's this?"

"Something Swordtail had."

Rentaro's eyebrows arched high. He gave it another close look.

"His phone was destroyed in the fight with Dark Stalker. This was about the only clue I could find on him."

Rentaro brought a hand to his chin in thought. "What's it for, you think...?"

"I have no idea." Hotaru sighed dejectedly, shaking her head. They debated the issue fruitlessly for a few moments before putting the topic to the side for the time being.

Next, Hotaru took a piece of paper out of her pocket.

"And this, too."

Rentaro took it, opened it up, and was shocked once more. It was Miori's analysis results from the Gastrea tissue sample. He stared at it, virtually boring a hole in it with his eyes. It was lined with rows and rows of unfamiliar-sounding chemical compound names. Just trying to read it gave him a headache.

"How're you supposed to read this?"

"I don't know any of the details, either. But Miori said *this* is what we should pay attention to."

She pointed at a corner of the sheet. Rentaro felt yet another jolt.

0.1 milligrams of trifdraphizin detected in Gastrea tissue.

A heavy shadow crossed over Rentaro and Hotaru. It was a train, roaring by at high speed across an overpass. It left nothing but silence behind.

"Trifdraphizin…?"

Hotaru's eyes fixed upon him. "You know that?"

Rentaro nodded, watching the stare of her blue-gray eyes from above her slender neck. "Hotaru, how much do you know about the Gastrea War?"

She shrugged, like it was the last question she expected. "Well, I'm part of the Innocent Generation, so the war's all just a secondhand story to me."

Rentaro closed his eyes and gingerly filed through his memories of the war.

It was a time of heady research, conducted at a breakneck pace in order to deal with all the Gastrea getting infected by the virus. Every sense of morals, or ethics, people had was hurled out the window. It was a wink and a nod on a global geopolitical level. People did pretty much anything you could think of—cluster bombing, chemical warfare, minefield laying, genetic engineering, human experimentation, you name it. The New World Creation Project was another spawn from that dark era.

"Does trifdraphizin have to do with that?"

Rentaro nodded. "Trifdraphizin was first reported on as this miracle drug that could suppress the propagation of the Gastrea Virus. There was this huge fanfare in the news when the announcement came out. It wound up never making it on the market. The effect was only temporary, and once an animal built up enough tolerance to it, it wouldn't work anymore. Still, there was one industry that still had a lot of expectations for it."

"Another one?"

"If you used it on people or Gastrea, they found that one side effect was that it induced a state of virtual hypnosis in them. There was a time for a while when black-market dealers would smuggle it out of the warehouse and sell it on the street as a date-rape drug."

The glories of academic research had a way of winding up like that. Finding uses far beyond anything their creators ever imagined. A bunch of mold eventually led to the discovery of penicillin, the first antibiotic. It saved millions of lives. Meanwhile, despite being created with noble aims, trifdraphizin found its real home in the underworld, dirtying the name of everyone involved with it.

The AGV test drug was like that, the "Anti-Gastrea Virus" compound Rentaro used to save himself after his encounter with Kagetane Hiruko caused half his stomach to get blown apart. It started as a failure, Sumire's doomed attempt to halt the spread of the Gastrea Virus, but later was used for other purposes.

"But why was that detected in the Gastrea tissue?"

"I don't know... Ever since it was banned from public distribution following that whole controversy, it's gotten a lot harder to receive approval to purchase any. I totally forgot about it, too. It hasn't shown up in the news in a while."

"Right, but you said it could hypnotize people, Rentaro? Does that apply to Gastrea, too?"

"Yep. It works on both. Of course, the Gastrea Virus eliminates and neutralizes just about anything that enters its host's bloodstream, so if you wanted long-term control over one, you'd need to have a hell of a lot of the stuff."

"Like, up to the point where it shows up in tissue analysis?"

Rentaro paused.

"Hang on. You really think so? What would the Five Wings Syndicate do with a bunch of hypnotized Gastrea? Or is that the Black Swan Project, or what?"

Hotaru silently shook her head. The main problem with this theory was the question of how Five Wings could get the huge supply of trifdraphizin this conspiracy would require. They would need connections for even a small amount. Underground connections. There was no way they could hide that kind of operation.

"Underground, huh?" he muttered to himself.

"You know someone, don't you?"

There was a sharp light in Hotaru's eyes.

2

Rentaro spent the next morning and afternoon recuperating. It was already nearly dark again by the time he set off. His destination: District 31 of Tokyo Area, part of the Outer Districts. It took several train transfers to get there.

By that time, in the year 2031, most of the Outer Districts were either abandoned or already down to rubble with no plans to renovate. However, the area that hosted Old Shinagawa Ward, Old Koto Ward, and Old Minato Ward was still relatively unscathed in comparison to some, being protected by the Monoliths that surrounded Tokyo Bay. As such, he knew it would make a good meeting point. Especially when the only people there would be local residents.

But he couldn't afford to rest easy. The person he was about to meet was part of the city's dark underbelly. He knew how easy it was to have a dead body "taken care of" in the Outer Districts, if it came to that. He'd prefer if it didn't.

Based on the address he was given, he anticipated a lengthy walk from the rail station to the meeting point. He wasn't expecting a march all the way to the edge of the Monoliths. At least the jet-black towers were still clear as day in the blackness. He certainly would not be getting lost.

Pushing his way through the crumbling infrastructure, eerie shadows flitting all around him, he finally heard the roar of the sea, accompanied by its telltale scent. Scrambling up a particularly large pile of rubble and surveying the landscape, he looked down at the mirrorlike black surface shining in the moonlight, the ripples in the water refracting the light this way and that. His heart lifted a bit at the rhythmical sound of the waves' advance and retreat. Then he spotted the far edge of the mammoth-size Monolith, sucking the very darkness into itself.

Climbing down and heading toward the oceanside wharf, he could see a line of elongated, semicircular warehouses lining the water. Comparing the signs to the number written on the scrap of paper in his hand, Rentaro eventually stopped in front of a storehouse, one notably larger than the rest.

Once upon a time, it was no doubt a seafood processing facility; there was no telling how much fresh fish and shellfish it handled in the past. The numbers painted on the wall were faded, almost succumbing to the constant barrage of salt-water air, but he could still tell he was in the right place.

Rentaro checked the time. Midnight. Nobody was there.

"So this is the sea..."

Wholly ignoring Rentaro's concern, Hotaru wandered toward the shoreline, a look of awe on her face.

"You've never seen it before?"

Hotaru looked up at him and nodded. "Can I go look?"

"Why do you need my permission?" Rentaro chuckled.

Under the blessed Monolith magnetic field, she could even go for a swim if she wanted, as long as she didn't wander too far offshore. However, given the seafaring Gastrea lurking somewhere under the surface in 2031-era Earth, seaside fun in the sun was usually seen as something reserved for the truly eccentric. The fishing industry was basically destroyed, and even missile-bearing ships with Varanium-lined bottoms could never be truly carefree on the high seas. Tokyo Area was now entirely reliant on shoreline spawning farms for their seafood, sending prices through the roof. *So it goes*, Rentaro supposed.

Forgetting about Rentaro for the time being, Hotaru ran to the shore. Then she stepped back a bit, surprised at the cold water and positively shocked at the sensation on the tip of her tongue after tasting it.

"Look, Rentaro! It's all salty!"

"Yeah, no shit!"

Her look of curious astonishment was as pure as it was childlike.

It shared something in common with Enju, and it forced Rentaro to recall how at odds he had been with *her*, too, when they first met.

"Are you okay, though? The Monolith's right nearby."

Initiator or not, she still had the Gastrea Virus coursing through her veins. Depending on her corrosion rate, that could have assorted effects on her.

"I'm fine," she replied. "My rate's still in the high teens."

"Oh. Well, there's *one* difference between you and Enju."

"What do you mean?"

"Nothing," Rentaro said as he glared at the sea, his thoughts turning elsewhere.

I swear I'll get you back, Enju.

Then he turned around, hearing the *thump* of feet against dirt behind him. A man was there, cool and composed as he walked forward. He was neither very young nor very old; in fact, it was hard to guess his age. He was in a completely white suit, and while his dull, sallow skin suggested he was well on in years, his eyes were quick, young, and penetrating. Rentaro's civsec instinct told him he was not to be trusted.

"You the guy Abe told me about?"

Rentaro kept his response to a silent nod.

Before they went there, Rentaro and Hotaru had paid a visit to Kofu Finance, the yakuza-linked loansharking outfit located in the Happy Building's fourth-floor office space. There, they had a little meeting. All of Rentaro's personal and business contacts were no doubt being marked by the cops at this point, but he doubted even they'd guess he had a yakuza friend or two. As it happened, he was right.

Shouki Abe, one of the mobsters he was familiar with, usually joked around with him whenever they met. But this time, he had acted oddly nervous. After some chitchat, he had borrowed a lighter, lit a cigarette, and seemed to noticeably calm down. "I was just surprised, Rentaro," he had admitted. "Your face has changed a lot."

It probably had. In order to avoid the facial-recognition cameras, Rentaro no longer let himself be caught in daylight without sunglasses. He had no time to shave, except for the bare minimum. Nor did he have time for a proper meal lately. Maybe it was showing in his hollowed-out cheeks.

Rentaro, dwelling on this, shook his head. That probably wasn't what Abe had meant, anyway. *This* Rentaro—formerly the pursuer, now the pursued, waiting for his chance to turn the tables on his enemy—probably *was* different. At least, it was to the point that it overwhelmed Abe at first glance, even though he was a man who had no doubt seen a thing or two in his line of work.

And to think that just a bit ago, I was being hailed as the hero of Tokyo Area.

It all seemed tremendously ironic. But he had pushed the thought away long enough to ask Abe about the recent market for trifdraphizin. The gangster had sourly explained it all to him. To sum up, the retail price for trifdraphizin was rising because of a lack of supply going around the market. Apparently some mystery group was buying it all up.

Abe had closed by promising to connect him to a courier better versed in the market than he. "Rentaro," he had said, "let me just tell you one more thing. I know we don't act like it sometimes, but there's a code of justice we all live by in here. Me, personally? I'm one hundred percent against the drug trade, period. Most of our people are just messing around with numbers on computers these days—insider trading, that sort of thing—but I think that beats drug dealing any day. That's the whole reason I'm here—I didn't wanna deal, so they demoted me to loansharking duty. So I'll help you, okay? But don't think that this makes you buddy-buddy with the Kofukai Group or anything. If you start messing around with our sources of income, I think you know how some of us are gonna react to that, you know what I mean?"

Rentaro ruminated over this previous conversation with Abe as he stared down the courier in front of him. The man, for his part, was focusing on the inky deep-black waters beyond the tetrapods scattered in the wharf, taking an occasional sideways glance in Rentaro's direction.

"So, what's the savior of Tokyo Area want to know?"

Rentaro ignored the verbal jab, giving the courier a cold gaze. "Who's going around buying up all the trifdraphizin on the market?"

"I can't really go around divulging information about my clients, now can I? Trust means everything in this business."

Rentaro was already fed up with this. Even someone like him—who preferred to let his guns do the talking instead of negotiate—could tell: This was *Abe's* way of sticking out his palm and asking for it to be greased.

"All right. Let's cut the crap. How much do you want?"

The man let out a raspy, vulgar laugh. "Well, if it's information you're looking for, this is about the going rate."

He had three fingers lifted up. *What a rip-off. You goddamned hyena.*

"I'll give you twice that. But it's gotta wait."

"You gotta be joking with me."

"I don't have it on me right now. Once I solve this case, I'll pay you double."

"Why do I have to believe an empty promise like that?"

"Hey, you can't collect from a dead man, right? So that way, I don't have to worry about you feeding me a line of BS intel. Besides, apparently I'm famous enough that even *you* know what I look like, so it's not like I can run from you for long."

"What if I say no?"

"Then only one of us is getting out of here in one piece. And lemme just say, I'm not exactly planning to die in a place like this."

The sea breeze beat against Rentaro's uniform and the courier's suit.

"I want triple."

Rentaro nodded. They had a deal.

"Okay. Talk to me."

The man removed a pack of cigarettes from his suit pocket and lit one of the sticks. The breeze blew the smoke toward the warehouse building.

"So actually, I don't really know much about the client, either. They send a negotiator over to work with me, but I don't go nosin' around in his business much. That's how it works, you know? It pays good enough, too."

"Come on," Rentaro interrupted, the irritation clear in his voice. The man raised a hand to stop him.

"Hang on. Lemme finish. Every time he makes a deposit, I deliver the trifdraphizin to a set location. It's kind of a weird one."

"A weird location?"

"Here in the Outer Districts, near one of the Monoliths, there's a path down under a manhole that looks pretty much like a coal mine. I open the manhole, climb down the ladder, drop off the stuff, and beat it. But I'm guessing that's their hideout."

Rentaro could feel a lightning-flash of inspiration erupt in his mind. "Hotaru."

The chestnut-haired girl next to him nodded deeply, holding in the excitement just as much as he was.

"We're finally on to something. That's gotta be a Five Wings Syndicate hideout, probably."

When Rentaro asked where it was, the man pointed out a spot in the Outer Districts that was almost exactly opposite theirs, the entirety of the city in between. It would take a while to get there. But they were ready.

Rentaro turned and began to walk off. "Whoa," a voice said. "What're you gonna do over there?"

"I thought you didn't go nosing around in client business."

"Well, judging by how much stuff they're ordering, the group you're pursuing probably has a lot of people working for it. I don't see anything besides handguns on you guys, but you sure you're ready to take on a group *that* big with just that?"

"What're you trying to tell us?"

The courier, diverging from his previous macho demeanor, shrugged.

"Oh, I'm just saying—if you die, I can't collect, you know? So I figure I could stand to up the ante a little bit. Follow me."

The man ventured into the truck loading dock of the nearby seafood plant, ducked into the management office, and went up into the building.

Rentaro and Hotaru exchanged glances.

"What do you think?" Rentaro asked.

"It's dicey, but I have to admit: We're short on resources. Let's try him."

So they followed along, about ten paces behind the courier as he navigated the hallways with a flashlight, not bothering to acknowledge them.

For an Outer Districts ruin, the processing plant was deteriorating in a remarkably orderly manner. Rentaro had seen dozens of abandoned buildings like this. He could sniff out the difference between a ruin that hadn't seen human activity in years, and a ruin simply made to look that way. His instincts told him this was the latter kind. Most useful buildings would have been long scavenged by the Outer District's denizens by then. This wasn't.

Going upstairs, the man stopped in front of a door, then held the flashlight with his teeth as he turned a crank. An airtight door for what was probably a freezer room opened up with a clang. The familiar scent of metal and machine oil flew out.

Taking a look inside made Rentaro sigh. It was, in a word, an arsenal. The walls were lined with countless numbers of handguns, hand grenades, assault rifles, and rocket launchers. They were all brand-new.

Rentaro shot a dumbfounded look at the courier. He shrugged again.

"Take whatever you like."

"Are you sure?"

The courier snickered nervously. "Lemme set something straight, though. I don't care about you. I care about you surviving long enough to pay me. Try not to confuse the two, all right?"

Rentaro nodded his thanks, then focused back on the arsenal. He brushed his hand against a nearby wooden crate. It felt moist. Using a nearby crowbar on the floor, he pried open the top of the box. There, encased in dried straw packaging and oiled paper, was a large cache of KRISS vector short-barrel machine guns.

"Ooh, here's a sniper rifle."

He turned around to find Hotaru grasping the large gun, arms trembling.

"An M24..."

It was the US Army's preferred choice of sniper rifle, a customized version of the Remington M700 they purchased in mass quantities. It was equipped with a Leupold 10x fixed-power scope. That made it the so-called A3 model, a heavily reworked version of the original. *Must have been sold off by the military. Amazing to see it here of all places*, Rentaro thought. *But hang on a minute—*

"You're gonna have to zero that. Otherwise you're not gonna hit the broad side of a barn."

"Oh? You know about these?"

"Ah," Rentaro replied, "we had a specialist over at the office. Can you handle that?"

"I'm still a student," Hotaru said, "but yeah. I'll zero this at one hundred meters. You want this?"

"Nah. I don't carry anything heavier than a handgun. Otherwise I'll just be a drag in hand-to-hand combat."

"Oh," Hotaru said, not particularly put off as she crossed her arms. "Well, if we can get some explosives over there, at least, that'll be perfect."

"Explosives?"

Hotaru stuck her hand into another crate and spread a set of rectangular hunks of clay—plastic explosives—on the floor. There were enough to practically start a war. Certainly more than enough to engage any enemy Rentaro could imagine.

By the time they were done casing the place, discussing their strategy, making their choices, and stepping outside of the building, the night sky was already starting to lighten. Day was breaking over the placid Pacific. Rentaro took a deep breath, then exhaled.

The duel was fast approaching.

3

"Oh. Swordtail was defeated as well...?"

"Yes. It was absolutely deplorable."

In a break room inside the Central Control Development Organization—the so-called "black building"—Hitsuma looked out the window toward the city, back turned to his conversational partner.

Yuga Mitsugi, watching his still-turned back, found himself confused. "I thought you'd be angrier than that," he said.

"I am," came the reply. "But before I gnash my teeth about it like a spoiled child, I wanted to think about how we're going to get Rentaro Satomi's head."

Yuga was impressed, although he decided not to mention this. Hitsuma was not the most satisfying boss he had ever worked with, but even he had matured a bit throughout this ordeal.

"I suppose one reason is that we looked down on Hotaru Kouro's powers. I couldn't pinpoint what kind of Gastrea factor she had, but the way Swordtail described it, she literally came back from the dead.

That, or her ability allows her to fake death, somehow, to throw her enemy off guard."

"How do we deal with that?"

It's about time you saw things my way, thought Yuga as he removed a rifle round from his pocket and rolled it across the table with a finger. The tip was black, the rest of the body a shiny brass. To Hitsuma, it looked like just another Varanium-tipped bullet. He turned around and scowled.

"*That's* your big strategy? Hummingbird had a Varanium knife; Swordtail had Varanium-tipped ammo. Look what that got them—"

"Hang on a moment, Mr. Hitsuma," Yuga said, raising a hand to interrupt. "The tip of this bullet contains enriched Varanium—metal that was melted down and concentrated. Upon impact, the Varanium inside bursts and spreads across the target's body. It's enough to kill any Gastrea up to Stage Three, as well as Initiators. It was a pain in the ass procuring these, lemme tell you."

"Stage Three?"

"You're familiar with that system, right? Targets you can kill with a normal Varanium weapon are classified as Stage One, and that covers most Gastrea and Initiators. If the target doesn't fall into that field, then we go up to Stage Two and beyond. With Stage Two, the Varanium keeps them from regenerating their bodies. You can still kill them if you decapitate or dismember them, or if you set them on fire. Stage Three, though, those guys can grow back arms and stuff. It's like being wounded causes their bodies' cells to call out to one another."

"Call out…?" Hitsuma said, eyebrows pressed farther down. Yuga grinned internally. It was exactly the response he'd expected.

"And Stage Four's even crazier. It can regenerate itself even if most of its organs are toasted. To kill them, you have to blow them to dust. That's the only way. That's the stage Aldebaran was at. Then, with Stage Five, you can put them in deep freeze, in a vacuum, toss 'em into molten lava running at two thousand degrees…but as long as the environment's right, they'll regenerate. Like, from the molecular level on up. Right now, in the year 2031, there's no physical way to kill them."

Hitsuma brushed a hand aside, fed up with the subject. "All right, all right," he said, eyes swiveled askance at Yuga from his handsome face. "I'm not here to listen to a bunch of gossip. So you're saying that bullet's good enough to kill Hotaru Kouro?"

"It's already in the bag, sir. At most, Hotaru would be Stage Two. No matter how good she is at regeneration, Stage Three's got to be the max."

"Hmm. Well. I would like to leave them to you...but I think we won't need those bullets you've gathered after all."

"What do you mean?"

"We might find Rentaro Satomi and Hotaru Kouro's hideout before long. We triangulated their general region based on their escape routes from the expressway shoot-out and the Shiba Heavy Weapons attack. I'm having my people sweep the streets."

Oh. Was *that* all?

"Even if you find them, sir," Yuga said as he shrugged and put his hands in the air, "no regular officer's gonna have a chance against them."

"Yes," Hitsuma agreed. "So I'm sending in civsecs."

Yuga found himself unconsciously narrowing his eyes. "...Civsecs?"

Hitsuma poured a paper cup of coffee from a nearby pot and offered it to Yuga. The assassin waved it away.

"I thought you weren't using them?"

He already had to cover up the total failure of the police to capture Rentaro at the Magata Plaza Hotel, despite the swarms of uniformed personnel on-site. That cover-up should have prevented him from enlisting civsecs or any other public service for this case.

"We can't be that picky any longer...in so many words."

"Who did you send over?"

Hitsuma paused to take a dramatic sip of coffee.

"A group perfect for the job, is who. They've already been briefed and are en route to the site. Sadly, you haven't been activated."

Yuga deliberated in silence for a moment. Then he quietly shook his head.

"I will be on standby for Rentaro Satomi at the time and place we discussed."

"Why would you do that?" a perplexed Hitsuma asked.

"...You've never traded blows with an opponent before, Mr. Hitsuma. I think this might be working on a dimension beyond your understanding. He's going to be there. I know he will."

At this, Hitsuma crossed his arms. Then he emptied the rest of the cup down his throat, apparently abandoning the effort, and tossed it in the bin. There was a *plip* as the cup joined the mountain of its kin down below.

"…You can do what you like."

Yuga nodded lightly. Hitsuma nodded back.

"Well, then…"

"Yeah."

That was all the good-byes they needed.

With a salute, Yuga left the break room and, by himself, took the first step to his final battle.

4

The jet-black sky rumbled its displeasure in semiregular intervals as it unfurled heavy, sharp rain upon the world. The sound of water slowly running along the gutter on its way down sounded like the steady current of a swampy river, uniting with the *drip-drip-drip* of rain wriggling its way through a roof leak and onto the floor, forming a watery ensemble.

Rentaro took in the sound as he lay down in the sculpture studio. It was humid, but the temperature had gone down a fair chunk. In Rentaro's mind, it certainly was more comfortable than the unrelenting heat he had to deal with over the past few days. Adjusting his position at all would send another billow of stone powder into the air, landing on him like dust, so he tried to remain as still as possible.

Lying there, unmoving, on the studio's bare floor, in total darkness with the windows shut, made him feel like a dead man. If he lay flat on his back and rested his hands on his stomach—it was like practicing for his stint in a coffin.

He had promised Hotaru that he would spend all day recuperating.

Part of him wanted to get up and rip the lid off the Black Swan Project right this second. The spirit was all too willing, incredibly willing, but the flesh could no longer keep up. Consuming the calories he needed had made the thoughts he knew all too well rev back into motion, but not his body yet. Still, he couldn't stop them. It was proving hard to forcibly shut down his thought process.

He marveled at it.

Part of the path to *satori*, the stage of enlightenment that was the ultimate goal of any Buddhist practitioner, involved training oneself to cast off all worthless thoughts from the mind.

He thought about that. But he also thought about Enju, who was bound to be paired with another Promoter sooner or later. As a civsec himself, he knew how difficult it would be to dissolve a pairing once it was set in stone. And once a Promoter was fully aware of the power within Enju, he'd never even think about letting her go.

It was hard to believe he hadn't seen her once since that last awkward conversation in the city jail. He wanted to see her with all his heart.

She had to feel constricted by now; she must have taken the media at face value, including the news that Rentaro was dead. The entire rest of the story had been shut away, for all he knew.

How is Tina doing, though? Even if she was made to go up on the stand and get convicted of something, it wouldn't happen that quickly. But between the judge, the prosecutor, her attorney, and even the jurors, it was hard to be optimistic. Being among the Cursed Children was hard to make up for.

If any semblance of human rights had been granted to Tina, then she was likely sitting in a corner of some jail cell, hands around her knees. A lifetime of being used and abused by corrupt adults... Rentaro couldn't stand having his friends put to public shame any longer. He wanted to protect her from all the hardships life had handed her.

Then Rentaro realized he was deliberately trying not to think about Kisara.

No. I haven't thought about anything. She was due to marry Hitsuma, *and I've completely frozen all thought about her, postponing any conclusion for some unknown time in the future.*

Things had gotten so bad for him because he had foolishly believed Hitsuma was a decent person. Because he left Kisara in his hands.

Then he felt the inner edges of his eyes grow warm. The tears accumulating on the outer edges crossed his cheeks.

I was wrong about everything.

How was he going to bow his head and say to her, *Cancel the marriage and go back home*? How, after he sent her away from the visitation room with all that vitriol? After he trampled all over her dignity?

There was a noise downstairs. Flustered, Rentaro wiped the tears from his eyes and pretended to be asleep.

After a moment, the nearby hinges creaked. Without turning his head, he could tell from the breathing that it was Hotaru.

"Rentaro, are you asleep?"

"...No, I'm up."

He carefully sat up as Hotaru shook the rain from her chestnut-colored hair and wringed out the hem of her tank top. He could see Hotaru's thin, bare, taut stomach. Her chest, drawn in the drape of the fabric over it, was visible through her undergarments.

Then, realizing she was being watched, Hotaru squatted down on the floor, hugging herself as she gave Rentaro a razor-sharp glare.

"Did you see me?"

Rentaro scratched the hair on the back of his head.

"Don't be stupid. Why would seeing a naked kid make me happy?"

Hotaru let out a long, deep groan. It was followed by a short sigh as she shook her head. "Take off your clothes. I need to change your bandages and wipe your body down."

She didn't bother to listen for a response before nimbly reaching behind him and removing his button-down shirt, stepping up to the noble task of wiping down his back.

Rentaro let her, feeling the cold, wet cloth against his skin.

Tomorrow was probably going to be the final battle, but he couldn't get the words to come out.

Somewhere along the line, Hotaru's attitude toward him had brightened considerably. The disdainful hostility of their first encounter was far gone now.

"You're wounded from head to toe."

"Ah, that's gotta be from the Third Kanto Battle. This is from the Seitenshi sniper, and I think Kagetane Hiruko put this one on me."

He pointed each one out like a general marking armies on a map. None were easy victories for him. The memories of each one were etched into his mind.

Then, unexpectedly, he felt something soft and slightly warm pressed against his back. It made him arch his spine.

It took him a while to realize it was Hotaru's cheek. "I'm sorry, Rentaro. I had the wrong idea about you."

Silence arrived out of nowhere.

Being together with her, even for this short time, taught him that behind all that curt bluntness was a little girl, one just as delicate as any other.

This can't go on...

Stealing a look at her from the side of his eyes, Rentaro made a decision in his heart.

"It's fine. Let's go to sleep."

He flicked the switch on the flashlight before she could respond. Then he lay back and used his crossed arms as a pillow. He could feel Hotaru looking at him for a moment, as if trying to say something, but then he heard the rustling of her clothes as she laid herself against the floor beside him.

Squinting into the darkness, Rentaro could just barely make out the white of the ceiling above them. His body was dead tired, but there was no way he could sleep now.

There was no telling how long he gazed upward. By the time the arms under his head went numb, he heard Hotaru turning over in her sleep.

It was just about time. He quietly got up.

Reaching into his back pocket, he took out a pen and notepad he had surreptitiously bought at the convenience store along with the flashlight. He ripped out a page, then—as well as he could in the darkness—wrote a note. He doubted his penmanship was much to brag about in this state, but he left it by Hotaru's side, quietly got to his feet, and tried to be as silent as possible with his footsteps.

Then he found himself illuminated. He raised a hand to cover his eyes.

"...Where are you going?"

Hotaru's voice was frigid.

"......"

There was nothing Rentaro could say. He silently returned Hotaru's gaze. Noticing the paper next to her, she picked it up and scanned it.

"...What's *this* about?" she said, sharpening her eyes and lowering the temperature of her voice even further. She usually spoke in an emotionless monotone, but now Rentaro could physically feel the anger. That was how in tune he was with her by this point.

"It's just like I wrote it. We're done, Hotaru. I wrote the whole procedure down. You go to the police and tell them I coerced you into cooperating with me. I don't know how far our enemy's infected the police, but you see Inspector Tadashima's name on there? He's at Magata Station. You can trust him."

"Stop screwing with me!"

"I'm not screwing with you."

"Are you running away from me?"

"I'm telling you to run away from me!"

He paused for a beat, breathing hard.

"...Hotaru, we're just barely still at the point where you can turn back. Honestly, one step away from it... Listen, I'm glad you believed me when I said I didn't kill him. I really am. Our enemy's so huge, it's got the police wrapped around its finger. Tomorrow's fight is gonna be so, so much worse than today's. And if you're with me for it, you're really gonna lose your life this time."

He tried to drum up some intimidation, some coercion in his voice. But Hotaru's response was beyond anything he could have anticipated.

"So you're just going to go away? Like Kihachi did?"

"What?"

Hotaru's face was despondent, her eyes blurred with tears.

"Kihachi did the same thing. He got all cold and distant with me one day. He started hiding lots of things. We kept working solo... I'd ask him, and he wouldn't say anything. My birthday was coming up, and I begged him to at least spend *that* with me, and it turned into this huge argument... When I woke up the next morning, there was a note by my bedside. He said he was gonna get everything squared away before my birthday. And it was right after that. When the police called and told me Kihachi was dead."

"That..."

It was an unimaginable thing to experience. Rentaro hesitated to give her some kind of halfhearted consolation.

"I still dream about what I should have done back then: That I was just pretending to sleep all along. That I followed Kihachi and shielded him from getting shot. That he kills the guy, and I apologize to him because I never had the chance the night before. That he holds me, and then he says in my ear, 'We're always gonna be together.'"

Hotaru shook her fists weakly.

"And then I wake up right there, every time. I'm in this bed that's too big for me, and it makes me grit my teeth every time. I swore that I'd protect my partner this time. Please, Rentaro! I want to come with you! I need to know! What happened to Kihachi? Why did he have to come back home like that? If I can't get revenge by being with you, I have to at least take a step toward my own future! Please, Rentaro!"

Their eyes locked and time seemed to stand still. Rentaro closed his own, then took a deep breath through his nostrils.

"All right, Hotaru. The hole that opened up in your heart after Suibara died... Let's fill it in together."

Hotaru's face grew brighter as she understood. She opened her mouth to speak but only ended up biting her lip. She hung her head low and muttered a simple "Thanks" instead.

It was almost as if she were crying tears of joy as she extended her right hand.

"I'm glad I got paired with you, Rentaro."

This must be the girl that exists deep down within her. Kinda cute when she smiles. Rentaro clasped his hand to hers. Her hand was unbelievably strong and steady for such a little girl, pulsating with warmth.

"So when's your birthday, anyway? Is it that close?"

"Oh yeah..." Hotaru took out her cell phone.

"We're right on time," she said as she showed the backlit screen to Rentaro. The time was twelve a.m.—midnight. She flashed a mischievous smile. "My birthday's today now. I'm ten years old."

This was going too fast. Rentaro searched his mind for some sort of congratulatory message he could give her; he had never quite gotten used to that kind of thing. So he scratched his head instead.

But then, a malicious intent made itself known behind them. Rentaro turned around, hand already at the grip of his Beretta. Hotaru noticed a moment later, eyes turning crimson as she released her own powers.

"Rentaro, are you there?" she whispered.

"...Yeah," he muttered back.

The sensation came from behind the door to the studio. Several sensations, in fact. But they didn't come through the door. They stood there, perhaps struggling with something themselves. Maybe they lost interest; maybe they decided to call for reinforcements. He didn't like it, but either way, holing up in the studio was no longer a good idea.

"Let's go. Follow me."

Signaling to his temporary partner, Rentaro readied his Beretta and tiptoed away.

The space they were squatting in was two stories high. It was far enough into the suburbs that the sound of battle wouldn't be an immediate cause for someone to phone the authorities. The rainstorm that rankled Rentaro's mind a few moments ago would help mute whatever happened as well.

Rentaro tiptoed behind a support column and went down the bare-concrete stairway. Taking a position adjacent to the front door, he dared a quick glance.

There were three figures, all standing there getting soaked by the rain. He strained to make them out through the beam of his MagLite, but when he finally did, his mind went blank. Before he knew it, he had forgotten about hiding, and exposed his body to the air.

"You guys… Why…?"

The three figures illuminated by the MagLite included a single tall man and two girls. The man wore a field jacket and a pair of amber sunglasses. The girl next to him was dressed fully in black, with a choker collar. The third, by comparison, was standing quietly, a girl in an armorlike exoskeleton.

Instinctively, Rentaro took a step beyond the building. The heavy rain immediately weighed down his clothes. He didn't even notice.

Because he knew each one of them.

They had walked the line between life and death together; battle comrades who constantly covered for one another. They were each worth an entire battle squadron by themselves.

"I was certainly not expecting to run into you again so soon."

The dignified voice belonged to Asaka Mibu, the girl in old-style armor. She took a step forward, her eternally closed eyes opened just a slit as she judged him with scorn. She was a warrior, one he had fought side by side with in the battle against Aldebaran. What was she doing here? She was unpaired… The IISO should have been taking care of her.

Asaka gave Rentaro another cold look, perhaps sensing his doubt.

"Thanks to the police pressuring the IISO, I am free from their control for the time being. I am ordered to dispatch a fiendish former civsec fleeing from the law after he committed cold-hearted murder."

The *tachi* sword she used to wield had now been replaced with a unique type of twin-bladed sword. A relic of her former Promoter, no doubt. She had it unsheathed and readied.

"I was looking forward to the day we would meet each other," she said. "But apparently the stars were not on our side after all. Prepare to die!"

Tamaki Katagiri, as if taking over for Asaka, similarly spat on the ground in Rentaro's direction: "The cops sent us a job. Not only did you kill a guy and run away, you bastard, but you were involved in the Shiba massacre, and that highway shoot-out, too! I saw the evidence!"

Rentaro was speechless. If the police were involved, Hitsuma was very likely pulling the strings. There was no telling what kind of contrived evidence he showed them, but something about the atmosphere indicated he wasn't talking his way out of this.

At the critical moment of the Third Kanto Battle, they had been laughing and crying with one another in turns. They had a friendship. And now Hitsuma had wrecked even that. Rentaro's murderous rage at the thought of that man thickened.

But another part of his mind was quickly analyzing the difference in battle position between the two sides, and it was driving him to despair. He had been their adjuvant leader. He knew full well what they were capable of.

"Rentaro, are these guys your…?"

Hotaru appeared next to him, a look of anxiety on her face. Rentaro gave her a firm nod. *There's nothing to worry about. Just fight with me for now.*

Asaka and Tamaki were livid; the trust they had built with Rentaro in the struggle against Aldebaran lay ruined. But there was one in the group that was not among their ranks. One with a conflicted look on her face.

"Why aren't you saying anything?" he asked.

It was Yuzuki Katagiri, her twin braids holding strong as she whisked her head back and forth. "Look at you. You're a filthy mess…! There's no way you can beat us! Please, just turn yourself in! I don't want to fight!"

"Don't taunt the prey. Catch it," Rentaro threw back.

"Huh?" Yuzuki asked.

"I'm saying, enough with this farce. I'm not giving up."

Across the way, Asaka's and Tamaki's expressions clouded; a look of disappointment crossed their eyes. Yuzuki, meanwhile, looked desperate as she took a step forward. "You…"

Rentaro raised his arms straight in front of him. His cybernetic one was out in all its glory.

Rentaro then deployed his mechanical eye. The pupil began to spin, creating a wave of geometric patterns.

"Come to think of it, I don't think I ever gave you my full intro," he said as he took the Tendo Martial Arts Water and Sky Stance and sized up his foes. "Give me a chance to before we start: I am Rentaro Satomi, of the Ground Self-Defense Force's Eastern Force; 787th Mechanization Special Unit, of the New Humanity Creation Project. I am ready to begin when you are."

"Ah…"

Yuzuki, still trembling, covered her face with one hand, looked up for a moment, then shielded it again. There was no fathoming the thoughts going through her head.

"Give it up, Yuzuki!" came the rebuke from her brother. That alone was enough to firm her resolve. The next time she raised her head, her face was hostile and unwelcoming.

The civsec group split off, going to the sides to surround Rentaro and Hotaru. A single signal was all it would take to set off the battle.

Rentaro knew he had no chance in an extended fight. If he wanted one, he had to strike first. In the back of his mind, all the memories of their time spent fighting and laughing together bubbled up from the void. Then, under the rain- and mud-soaked pant leg that concealed it, a cartridge in his leg propelled him forward.

5

Sometime before Rentaro thrust himself into battle…

The rain was coming down in buckets, but it still wasn't enough to wash away the smell of alcohol that permeated the entire street.

The red and green streetlights cast their clouded illumination through the rain. He had bumped umbrellas, or nearly bumped them, with several staggering drunks on the walk. The touts attempting to lure him into nightclubs and bars, their tenacity going well beyond what city regulation allowed, were starting to irk him. If he had his policeman's uniform on, that would have snapped all these intoxicated people out of their drunken stupor. As a plainclothes inspector, however, he wasn't given the chance to unfold the old hat and blue pants all too often.

Holding the umbrella between his neck and shoulder, Shigetoku Tadashima unfurled a full-size road map—a rarity these days—and searched for his destination. Once he successfully spotted it, he turned his face up and took a look at the building across from him through the pounding rain.

"…This is it?"

He wasn't entirely sure he was correct, but then he saw TENDO CIVIL SECURITY AGENCY in block lettering on the third floor.

What a pile this is, he couldn't help but think. This man that people hailed as the savior of Tokyo Area, running an office in the shabby outskirts of town—someplace where even a strip club would hesitate to set up shop. He doubted the person he was looking for would be in at this time of night, but given that her home address turned up nothing, this was the only lead he had.

Folding up his umbrella and batting the handle against the ground to shake off water, he climbed up to the third floor. There was a frosted glass door, TENDO CIVIL SECURITY AGENCY stamped on the nearby wall panel. He rang the bell. Then he did it twice more. No response.

He was just about to turn back toward the stairwell when his eyes detected movement somewhere beyond the frosted glass. "Excuse me?" he called out, tapping on the door again. "I'm visiting from Magata Station."

His patience was rewarded. After another moment or two, he heard a click, then was greeted by a young woman in black.

"Um, what time do you think it is right—?"

The banter cut off. A look of vague recognition emerged on the woman's face.

"Inspector…Tadashima, right?"

Tadashima saluted in response. "I apologize for calling on you late at night," he began, following standard procedure. "Would you mind if I took up a little bit of your time? I wanted to ask you about the Rentaro Satomi case."

Kisara seemed to ponder this for a moment. Then she stepped back and opened the door fully, inviting him in. Taking a closer look, Tadashima realized she was in a black negligee. He must have woken her up after all. It was basic—no frills or lace or whatnot—but it wasn't the kind of thing even a grown woman would wear around a stranger.

She didn't seem to care, however, as she walked with an unsteady gait toward the kitchen. Her blank, glassy eyes had a dangerous fragility to them—just one touch seemed enough to make them shatter—but they also held a passive sort of beauty that didn't resist one's gaze. *She is beautiful*, Tadashima thought. He could understand why Rentaro got so passionate about her. But something bothered him.

He had run into her several times during investigations from the Hiruko terror attack forward, but the Kisara he remembered was always standing up to her full height, arms crossed and acting miffed about something or other. The haughty girl of his memory wasn't the one who had just greeted him. He wondered if he'd misremembered something.

Then, in the dark room that smelled of mold, he noticed another thing that didn't quite match the scene: a headless mannequin next to the office desk in a pure white wedding dress. A top-of-the-line one. The price could've easily broken ten million yen.

"I'm getting married."

Startled, he turned around to find Kisara emerging from the kitchen with some teacups on a tray.

"…I apologize for asking, but how old are you?"

"Sixteen."

"Ah… Well, no problem from a legal perspective, anyway. What are you going to do about school, though?"

"I'm dropping out," came the flat, stiffened reply. Her half-averted eyes were pointed at Tadashima's feet, as if she had resigned herself to the whole affair. Tadashima's instincts warned him against pursuing this any further, but his detective's curiosity won out.

"When's the big day?"

"Um, it's tomorrow. Hitsuma…I mean, my fiancé, got everything together at breakneck speed. He insisted."

Tadashima couldn't believe his ears.

"Hitsuma? You said Hitsuma just now, right?"

"Yes…"

"You don't mean Superintendent Atsuro Hitsuma from the department by any chance, do you?"

"Do…you know him?"

"Do I *know* him? Well…"

Now Tadashima was on the verge of forgetting what he had come there for. Hitsuma never even gave the slightest hint that he was about to become a wedded man—and it was tomorrow? *That* fast? With a *sixteen*-year-old?

Is Mr. Hitsuma hiding this marriage from the public? But why?

Kisara stood up, opened a drawer in her ebony office desk, and returned. There was a gold pocket watch in her hand. Opening the cover, the watch face glittered like the Milky Way, jewels festooned across it. It took only one glance to see how exquisite the timepiece was.

"When it was settled between myself and Mr. Hitsuma…he gave this to me. It's nice, you know? Not having to worry…about money, and things."

There was not even a faint echo of happiness in her voice. It seemed like she was talking to herself more than Tadashima, attempting to shoo some lingering regret out of her mind. Tadashima wasn't sure how to respond, so he took a teacup to his lips, tried a sip—and winced.

"Um…I'm sorry for being rude and all, but you made this tea with water, right?"

"Huh?" For a moment, the spark of reason returned to Kisara's filmy eyes, her cheeks blushing. "Oh, no, I messed it up again… Oh, and I greeted a guest wearing nothing but this…! I'm so stupid."

Without warning, her face twisted. She brought both hands to it. "I hate it."

"What?"

She finally broke, Tadashima thought as her body began to tremble.

"I hate it… Really, I…I don't want to get married to Mr. Hitsuma. I—I want to see Satomi. Satomi… He… Why did he have to die?"

Now the story behind this unnerving scene made sense.

Hitsuma, for reasons he couldn't surmise, was hiding Rentaro's continued existence from Kisara. She saw what had happened at the Plaza

Hotel, and from that, she thought he was dead. And no one had told her otherwise.

This was starting to make him incredibly furious. Yes, he knew it hadn't been reported in the news. The reputation of the police department was at stake. He was enough of a lifer in the force to put up with those sorts of politics. But she was practically family to the guy. Shouldn't Hitsuma have at least told *her* the truth, as long as she promised to keep it under wraps? And now he was forcing his hand in marriage on a woman who barely qualified as an adult? What was he thinking?

Tadashima opened his mouth. The truth had to come out—

But the logical side of his mind stopped him. Doing this, it screamed, would be an act of open rebellion against Atsuro Hitsuma. Tadashi Hitsuma, his father and main backer in the force, was the commissioner of the whole police department. The big boss. If he did anything to draw his attention, Tadashima could be drummed out of there the very next day.

But if he shut his mouth now, he was sure he'd regret it for ages to come.

What you're doing is wrong, *Mr. Hitsuma.*

Tadashima placed both elbows on the glass top of the reception-room desk, took a deep breath, and exhaled.

"President Tendo, I want you to listen carefully to me. The police have been hiding it in order to cover up their mistakes, but Rentaro Satomi is still alive."

A crash echoed across the room. Kisara froze, the teacup falling helplessly out of her hand.

—Then, as if waiting for that exact moment, they heard a much gentler sound from somewhere. A familiar melody, the pure sound of musical iron keys being plucked by a mechanism. It was a music box.

He didn't have to search long for it.

"Why is that...?"

Tadashima stared at it, sitting there on the desk, then searched out the wall clock. It was exactly midnight.

BLACK BULLET 6 CHAPTER 05

PURGATORY STRIDER

1

Rentaro's life-and-death battle, playing out over dirty mud puddles, was turning into a desperate nightmare.

Having faced off with them once in the past, he was fully aware of the Varanium chainsaw wrapped around the gauntlet worn by Tamaki Katagiri, as well as the "territories" his sister Yuzuki could make with her invisible wires. What threw him off his game the most, however, were the immensely powerful slashes unleashed by the tiny body of Asaka Mibu. Her "twin sword" had a single handle, from which extended two blades, one in each direction. It was a bizarre sight, and one about the length of a typical spear—but the blades, which spun in the air as Asaka twisted her hips in a sort of lethal dance, let her land two blows with a single swipe. He had to be careful around it. The shock waves that fanned out whenever she beat the blades against the ground were akin to a localized tremor as well, enough so to force him to brace himself.

Yuzuki and Tamaki always chose that moment to lunge upon him, too. The chainsaw screamed each time it whizzed past his ear.

He and Hotaru had tried launching a tandem barrage to at least get Asaka out of the picture. It was met with a flurry of sparks and zinging noises as she deflected it, spinning her weapon like a propeller. It floored him to see it in action.

Come to think of it, her IP Rank *was* 275, wasn't it? Following Tina and Kohina, she was the third highest-ranked Initiator Rentaro had ever met in his life. There was no way he could treat her lightly.

Meanwhile, he was starting to get a read on her innate ability as well. Whatever her Gastrea factor was, it was geared for power—power further enhanced by her armored exoskeleton. The kick Rentaro uncoiled with all his spinal strength was stopped by the shock-absorbent fibers woven into the armor, barely damaging her at all.

His main means of survival in this battle were the one-shot finishers he could unleash by discharging his leg cartridges. But his foes knew about that. And whenever he set himself up to let one off, they would promptly take their distance from him.

This time, there was no relying on Hotaru's miraculous regeneration skills. If Hotaru left the battlefield for even a moment, it'd be three-on-one, which meant Rentaro would be dead. She must have known this. She was keeping a safe distance from the enemy at all times, putting herself mainly in a backup-fire role. But if you ignored her regeneration, Hotaru's basic skills were a far cry from both Asaka's and Yuzuki's.

There was no conceivable path of victory. It was a situation where anyone would've immediately assumed the end was near. But Rentaro's confrontational tenacity made Tamaki and his team honestly gaze in wonderment.

"Why?!" screamed Yuzuki, who should have had a decisive advantage but instead found herself brushing away her rain-soaked hair in wonderment. Rentaro had used his cybernetic eye to dodge Asaka's three-slash twin-sword strike by a hair's breadth, all while using his artificial leg and arm to deflect Tamaki's chainsaw knuckle and Yuzuki's kick. He now planted that leg on the ground. It sank in a little as he gritted his teeth.

"*Ohhhhh!*"

He thrust it down with all his might as the Katagiris wavered. At the same time, he triggered a cartridge. It kicked downward, allowing him to stomp on the earth with enough force to compress the dirt underneath. His leg gouged a hole in the muddy ground, and the next moment, the earth shuddered.

Asaka realized what he was doing soon enough to step away. Yuzuki and Tamaki did not. They fell to the ground, kicking up mud. Without a second thought, Rentaro dashed forward for a follow-up. If he didn't beat Asaka, there would never be any victory for him.

By the time she lifted her twin sword high and sent it zooming down, she and Rentaro were a good twenty meters away from each other. He thought she had misjudged his advance by a fairly wide margin, but a chill suddenly ran up his spine. In an instant, he tilted his trajectory to the side.

It was just in time to hear a horrendous shredding sound that made his back feel cold with terror. The earth Rentaro had stood on just a moment ago was cleanly cut in two.

It unnerved him. That slash had some serious distance to it. And unlike Kisara's, it had made a clean slice through ground like it was made of butter.

The second strike that came at him was parallel to the ground. Rentaro ducked under it; a moment later, another shredding sound erupted behind his back. He turned around without stopping, only to find the second floor of the sculpture studio crumbling behind him, belching soot and smoke as it did.

He ran, gritting down hard on his teeth until he cried out in pain. Asaka was getting closer and closer. Once he was within range of her sword, the blades began to spin like a tornado, forming ever-changing arcs in the air as they carved the earth under his feet.

Rentaro's eye made calculations at blazing speed. He desperately struggled to read the blades, dodging the second strike, feinting, and making a wide leap to the right. Asaka flashed a look of surprise.

Now!

He tried to unleash an all-or-nothing cartridge from his leg—but then he lost his balance, as if pulled up by some unseen hand.

Rentaro checked behind him. His eyes opened wide.

"Oh, shi—"

There was a spider's web, a shining rainbow as it stood illuminated by the arched streetlight. It was being pulled by Yuzuki, hatred clouding her face as she remained on the ground. Rentaro had been caught in it when he stopped her kick with his right arm.

But there was no time to gnash his teeth about it. Asaka's twin blades were on their way, ready to skewer him.

Rentaro closed his eyes. *I didn't make it.*

There was a loud, shrill *vween* as the blades flew.

And continued to fly...away.

No one was more surprised to see this than Asaka herself.

A bullet had flown in from somewhere, making a clean hit on the extended blade. It shot sparks into the air as it knocked the weapon clear from her hands. And that wasn't all. Another bullet, launched at almost the same time, tore through the spider web as well, its heat loosening the strands.

The accuracy of both shots was incredible.

"Rentaro!"

Before Hotaru's voice could even reach his ears, he started moving. Rentaro dove toward Asaka's chest. The light around him swerved and spun—light that came from the explosion set off by his leg cartridge.

Asaka's expression, which he saw just a glance of, resembled a child lost in an amusement park. She was at a total loss.

Ten minutes later, Rentaro stood amidst the mud and grime, letting the rain plink down upon him.

Two people were strewn around him. There was Asaka Mibu, lying facedown in a mud puddle like a worn-out paper bag detached from her shattered exoskeleton. On the other side was Yuzuki Katagiri, lying on her back.

"*Nnhh...* Shit... This is crazy."

Rentaro turned toward the coughing voice. Tamaki was leaning hard against the wall, wiping blood from his mouth.

It was just as he'd hoped. Once Asaka was down, Tamaki's and Yuzuki's weaknesses were fully exposed to the world. They were well aware of the instantaneous force his cartridges gave him—but Rentaro was just as aware of their tactics.

Both were geared for close-quarters combat. Tamaki and his pistol could handle mid-range ops as well, but the Magnum he used, while powerful, had serious recoil issues and couldn't store many bullets at once. It was almost entirely meant for Gastrea engagement. Compared to Rentaro's Beretta, which relied on strength in numbers ammo-wise, it would be wholly useless in a shoot-out.

If Rentaro and Hotaru went full-fire on Tamaki, Yuzuki would naturally have to fly in to protect him. Then it'd be a matter of wearing her out. It didn't take a military genius to come up with that plan. And it went without saying that Tamaki going at it solo had no chance at all.

Tamaki lifted his head. Rentaro could see, through the amber frames, that his eyes were full of murderous hatred for the traitor before him. Rentaro eyed him coldly.

"*Eat* it!"

Then he buried his fist in his stomach.

Tamaki groaned, whispered "God damn it" to himself, set his head down, and fell unconscious. Rentaro looked at him for a few moments, then closed his eyes and stood quietly in the sprinkling rain.

"Rentaro…"

He turned around to find Hotaru looking up at him, hands crossed against her chest in concern. He shook his head and passed by her side.

"Let's go. It's too dangerous here."

He still had work to do. If he could reveal the Black Swan Project to the world, all this effort would be worth it—no matter how much hatred and how many muttered curses he had to take along the way.

2

Using his hand to shade his eyes, Rentaro looked up. The rising sun from the east was half-blocked by the enormous wall in front of him, but already the heat it cast out was beating against his skin.

NO. 0013 was stenciled on the bottom of the wall. It was a Monolith, an edifice of black chrome. Rentaro and Hotaru had spent the night traveling to it, taking the long way to evade detection.

Turning around, he surveyed the ruined buildings and piles of rubble. They extended out as far as his eyes could see. Around them, tilted electric poles provided weak support for wires that snaked out in all directions, like a giant game of cat's cradle. The only fortunate thing about the sight was that it was still far too early for the Outer Districts' denizens to be out and about.

"This is it?"

"Yes. I'm sure of it."

Hotaru's reply came in her usual suppressed tone, although Rentaro could sense a hint of excitement.

"The courier said there should be a manhole somewhere here. Let's look for it."

The ground beneath them was lined with aluminum cans and piles of colorful, dew-covered plastic garbage. Rentaro hardly wanted to touch any of it, so he kicked it away instead. It was oddly warm, as if decomposing. Yet it was a seemingly endless pile of materials, mortar, rusty nails... Finding actual soil proved to be difficult.

Just when they began to wonder if the courier fed them a line after all, Rentaro spotted a brand-new manhole cover amid the junk. He called Hotaru over and showed it to her. "That's gotta be it," she immediately replied.

"How do you know?"

She used a foot to point out the area next to the cover. There was a tiny star mark with wings, small enough that it was easily overlooked. He could feel his blood vessels tense in response.

Allowing Hotaru to hoist off the cover and toss it aside, Rentaro felt a cold wind run up his spine, along with the tingling smell of some kind of filth. Pointing his light downward, he saw a rusted-out pipe and corridors leading left and right.

The two threw their weapons-laden traveling bag and aluminum case inside, quieted the voices in their minds telling them to stay back, and took the rusted ladder one step at a time. Rentaro took the lead, although he wasn't enthusiastic about it. Leaving the sun above them like this made it feel as though they were pacing right into the maw of some enormous monster.

It was, of course, dark inside. The only light they had to work with was the MagLite's small circle. There was an ever-present whistling groan, like the wailing of the dead. *Just the wind crossing some kind of hollow crevice*, Rentaro told himself.

Hotaru flashed the light down one side, then the other.

"So we got the Monolith on one side and the way we came from on the other. Which way?"

"Which way would you go?"

"The way we came."

"Okay. Let's take the Monolith direction."

Hotaru gave him a kick in the shin. It actually hurt a fair bit. "You are so *stupid*!" she said, cheeks puffed up.

Rentaro gave an apologetic chuckle. "Well, let's just try going toward the Monolith first, okay? If it's a dead end, we'll go back the other way."

She nodded after a moment, not seriously offended after all.

The slushy liquid around their feet gave an odd, swampy *shlorp* with every step they took. The echoing grew louder the closer they came to the Monolith, making the waves of worry crash loud against their minds.

The path curved gradually at one point, but was otherwise basically a straight shot. After about one hundred meters, Rentaro and Hotaru stopped.

"Dead end…huh?"

A large wall about a meter across stood before them.

They hadn't been counting every step, but chances were that they were now directly underneath the Monolith. That would explain why the wall was black chrome, shining brightly in the flashlight's beam. It must have been to block the Gastrea.

"Guess you chose wrong, huh?"

"Um, I think it's too early to say that."

"Rentaro?"

Hotaru, already on her way back, turned around. Rentaro ran a hand against the smooth, cold surface of the Varanium wall. His fingers came across a depression.

He instructed Hotaru, standing beside him, to touch it. Surprise ran across her face. There was a hole in the Varanium, not even two centimeters across.

"Remember that loud whistle we heard? I knew the wind had to be coming in through somewhere. But look—"

Rentaro fell silent and pointed the light straight ahead.

"Doesn't this look like a keyhole to you?"

The quizzical Hotaru brought a shocked hand to her mouth, then hurriedly fumbled in her jacket.

"I got it."

She took out the key with the maple leaf—the one Swordtail had owned. The one whose home they had no clues about. The mystery.

Rentaro took a step back as Hotaru inserted the key and twisted it. There was an ever-so-slight click, and then it silently opened, beckoning them in.

"Holy…!"

A domed space, about the size of a small home, had been dug into the earth. Stationed inside of it was something that looked like a train. A bit of a small one—and a bit too large to be a microbus—but close enough.

"A light-rail line…? Why's there one here?"

They walked through the door, only to find the ceiling was higher up than they expected. They could see the tracks the train car was on now, extending deeper into a tunnel. They tried shining the light down the way, only to be greeted with total darkness. It *must* have been a light-rail station.

"I guessed right…"

"Uh-huh."

It seemed safe to guess that the Five Wings Syndicate was perched on the other side of the tunnel. Considering they were right under the Monolith, boarding this car would take them into the Unexplored Territory.

These guys had cornered the market on trifdraphizin, the same drug Rentaro and Hotaru had found in that Gastrea. They had killed Kihachi Suibara, Ayame Surumi, Kenji Houbara, Saya Takamura, and Giichi Ebihara. And those were only the names Rentaro knew. He understood full well they were just the tip of the iceberg.

What had those victims known? Why did they have to be murdered? What was the Black Swan Project—this menace that consumed the blood of so many people, this presence that must have been straight ahead?

Carefully, the two approached the rail car, all but expecting a trap as they boarded. It was...a train car. Eerily so, right down to the seating and the leather straps dangling from the ceiling. There wasn't a spot of dust inside, and it felt like the car had seen use fairly recently.

Rentaro turned to the driver's seat, wondering how the thing worked. He was rewarded with a set of instructions placed right on the instrument panel. After a quick once-over, he was convinced driving it was within his grasp. The key was already in the ignition; he twisted it, the engine revved to life, and the headlights—far brighter than the MagLite he was working with—cut through the darkness. Then he placed his hands on the cold, metallic master-control handle and gradually pushed it up. With a shudder, the speedometer began to ratchet upward, the handles on the ceiling swaying back and forth.

Bringing the handle up to gear P5, Rentaro watched as the car switched to running on momentum, maintaining a steady fifty kilometers an hour. Turning behind him, he saw Hotaru glued to a window, staring at the tunnel's inside. "I think the tunnel walls are made of Varanium," she said.

Rentaro focused on the tunnel to confirm it for himself. "I see. They must've used a shield to dig this hole."

"A shield?"

"A tunneling shield. You know, one of those big borers with a cutter bit on the end of it. These days, you have machines that bore the tunnel while laying down wall segments behind it, reinforcing it so it doesn't collapse. They probably used Varanium segments on this."

"That's pretty amazing," Hotaru blithely replied. But Rentaro sensed she had something else to say. He had a pretty good idea what it was, too. The Five Wings Syndicate used a tunneling shield to dig this pathway; they clearly maintained it well; they had laid rails across it; and now they had a working train system. Any way you sliced it, this was a huge job.

There was a proposal making the rounds called the Cassiopeia Project that would link all five Areas in Japan via underground trains. But not only was that a huge engineering challenge; it was also being heavily lobbied against by assorted vested-interest groups, balking at the idea of cheaper goods or produce from other Areas flooding the market. To say the least, it would be a long time coming. But an entity like the Five Wings Syndicate taking the initiative and building something like this? How large a group *was* this, anyway?

As they drove on in silence, Rentaro heard the sound of wheels grating against track as the car shifted slightly. He kept his hand on the control handle, peering into a darkness so black not even the headlights could penetrate it. Then he heard a clank behind him. He twirled around, only to find Hotaru opening up their luggage and preparing for battle.

"Rentaro," she said as she pulled the cocking handle back on a KRISS vector machine gun and squinted at the chamber, "I was thinking—we probably shouldn't help each other out in battle after all. If I get taken down, just keep on fighting, okay? I'll try to do the same thing."

Her tone was blunt, just like it was when they first met. Rentaro opened his mouth to object, but before he could, he asked himself why she was acting like this now, of all times. Maybe she was thinking that something could happen to her in the not-too-distant future, depending on what was waiting up ahead.

Spotting a stop sign marked in red, Rentaro hurriedly turned the handle toward the brake section. He lurched forward, then rocked back when the car finally stopped.

"We're here."

At the exit was a simple concrete floor with a rust-colored door on the other side. Above it was a lit-up green sign, a bit like Japan's standard emergency-exit signs, except this one read BIOCHEMISTRY LABORATORY #3.

"A laboratory?" Rentaro said. "Here?"

"Where do you think we are on the map right now?"

"Well, we've been going fifty kilometers an hour for twenty or so minutes, so simple math says we've traveled around sixteen kilometers."

They were certainly well into Unexplored Territory, beyond the protection of the Monoliths. Was this some kind of underground lab, then? If they had any facilities on the surface, how did they keep them safe from Gastrea attack?

Rentaro wiped his sweaty palms on his pants, put a hand on the doorknob, and took a glance at Hotaru.

"Let's go in."

He opened the door and walked through.

It was dim. The ceiling lights that connected to the outside corridor shone a light blue like will-o'-the-wisps, reflecting off the silvery gray walls and floor. It reminded Rentaro of a hospital after lights-out. Nobody was around, although he could hear the hum of some kind of machine operating. It smelled like medicine, too. The floor was immaculate; someone had clearly cleaned it recently.

Going through a set of double doors, Rentaro found himself in a locker room. On one wall, he found what looked like an attendance sheet. On it were plates with names like Firebird, Huckebein, and Squid Octopus—no real names at all. All the movable tags were turned around, indicating that no one was currently on duty.

But he doubted they were all on vacation. In fact, chances were the Five Wings Syndicate had abandoned the lab because they were fearful of Rentaro's advance.

That hunch was all but confirmed when he entered the adjacent business office. It was littered with piles of cross-shredded paper and ash—presumably they started burning paper when the shredding didn't go fast enough. Apparently paper was still being used as a trusted data format around there.

Five Wings must have known by then that Rentaro defeated Hummingbird and Swordtail, he reasoned. They must have figured this site was his ultimate destination, so they'd vacated. And if that reasoning was right, there was nothing there for Rentaro to discover.

And yet, opposing his logic was the feeling that something was nearby. Like someone was holding his breath in the darkness, constantly staring at him.

The elevator they came across next seemed to be powered, but for some reason, both Rentaro and Hotaru instinctively resisted boarding the eerily bright car. From the button panel, they learned that the facility had one aboveground floor and two basement stories. They decided to take the stairs down to the bottommost floor.

There, they found a sterilization room apparently meant for disinfecting *people*. Protective clothing hung from hooks on the wall, but Rentaro wasn't too interested in following procedure at the moment. Opening up the bulkhead door on the other side, he discovered that it led to another, even thicker door, the surface of which resembled space station materials. It opened on cue after the door they just went through closed.

The room beyond opened up into a fairly wide hallway where, in the darkness, they saw something odd ahead.

"Are these...cages?"

Rectangular cages, built into the corridor walls, lined both sides of the path. They continued down the hallway as far as they could see, but what struck the pair as particularly odd was their size. These were nothing like the tabletop cages to house lab rats or rabbits. They were far bigger, and they could faintly hear the sound of breathing coming from them. Something was there. And not just one or two things.

Rentaro could feel them staring at him with bated breath.

He took a step forward, only to feel something pulling him back by his shirt. He turned to find Hotaru shaking her head at him. He knew painfully well why she was doing that, but he also knew there was no going back now.

"Lemme go see what it is," Rentaro said as he began to softly walk down the hallway, seized by regret that felt like leaving his planet for another. He tried looking into a cage, but in the darkness he couldn't make out what was huddled in the far corner.

With shaky hands, he illuminated the nearest cage with his MagLite. A creature with blood-red eyes immediately reacted by shrieking and making a mad dash for the cage wall. It slammed itself against it repeatedly, emitting ear-piercing screams as its razor-sharp teeth chewed at the bars.

A panicked Hotaru responded by spraying fire from her short-barrel machine gun.

"*Screeeeee!!*"

The creature, emitting a noise like a mouse being strangled to death, fell back to the other side of the cage. This was followed by an eerily loud scream, as if the walls had just exploded. The creatures in the other cages, excited by the gunfire, were now copying their dead companion's act, screaming and bashing themselves against the cage bars.

"Let's move!"

Rentaro didn't bother to wait for Hotaru's reaction as he grabbed her hand and dashed down the hallway. He hit the door at the end with his shoulder, as if attempting to batter it open. He turned around, breathing heavily.

"Was that…really…?"

"Yeah."

He waited for his pulse to slow, then gingerly approached a cage and lit it up again. Bodies shone in the light, thanks to the viscous slime covering their skin. They smelled like rotting flesh, spitting something sticky at him as they screamed at the top of their lungs, as if casting a curse upon him.

"Are these Gastrea?"

"Look at that…"

Rentaro pointed his light not at the Gastrea, but at the cage. Hotaru's body tensed up, as if she had been shot.

"Varanium cages…? You're kidding me. Why…?"

All Gastrea had a natural fear of Varanium, to the point where locking them in a room lined with the metal on all sides would make them grow weak and die. The laboratory had probably been abandoned for at least a few days, but these creatures would have been in the cages for longer than that. Even a Stage Four Gastrea would have been half-dead by now. So why were they still alive?

All Rentaro could do was file the question away for later as he continued on.

Inside of a small room meant for handling dangerous P4-level biohazards, they found an octopuslike monster, its tentacles twisted and bony. It shrieked at them, too, repeatedly slamming itself against a glass window.

A door with the sign OPERATING ROOM led to what looked like a crime scene. Looking at the state of the thing on the operating table, Rentaro immediately shut the door. This room, at least, was skippable for him.

It seemed clear that this lab was being used for assorted types of Gastrea experimentation. The researchers must have been in such a hurry to evacuate that they didn't even take the time to euthanize their test subjects. Yet, despite all the dreadful scenery he had seen so far, Rentaro was still nagged by the feeling that he still hadn't reached the main section. He needed to know about the Black Swan Project, and there had to be something there that'd bring him to the root of it.

After taking a full tour of the facility, they concluded their journey in front of a door a fair bit larger than the others. According to the map on a wall they happened upon, it opened to a large space, about the size of a concert hall. A plate on the side read CULTIVATION ROOM.

"Let's go in," Rentaro said as he fiddled with the control panel to the side of the door. Inside was another bulkhead door; it whirred open with a hydraulic *psshh*, and with it, Rentaro felt a blast of cold air hit him from below.

Once the air cleared, it came into view: a room full of large, jellylike masses. Akin to yellow bags that someone had inflated into a ball, they squirmed around like a baby in the womb. A mesh of blood vessels ran across their surfaces, densely crisscrossing over one another, as they hung ponderously from the domed ceiling.

Each one was just large enough to house a grown human. The bags were thin and transparent, and inside were what appeared to be a large number of half-man, half-fish creatures, as well as a large beetle with a thick, warty carapace, a ropelike creature that looked like something in between a snake and a roundworm, and assorted other living things.

As crowded as the room was with them, the yellow bags looked a bit like gigantic muscat grapes, hanging in bunches from the ceiling—each one with a Gastrea inside. Like purple wisteria trees laden with grapes.

"She had to burn the vineyard."

Even though they had never met, the voice of Dr. Surumi rang softly in Rentaro's mind.

"This…," Hotaru whispered. "This is crazy. It can't be real."

"Well…believe it."

Hotaru must have known it by then; she was just pretending not to. For some reason, her professed disbelief made Rentaro furious.

"They're *raising* them! They're raising Gastrea in here! And not just any Gastrea, either…"

He knew letting his anger out on Hotaru wasn't constructive at all. But the pure, unadorned horror seizing him made it impossible to control.

"The Gastrea they care for in here get put into those cages we saw once they reach maturity. These aren't normal Gastrea… They're making them so they're immune to Varanium. *That's* why being in a Varanium cage doesn't kill them. God… So *this* was it the whole time?"

Sumire had said it herself: "*Swans, you know, are supposed to be all white in color, but then they found a population of black swans in Australia. It turned the world of ornithology upside down back in the day. The entire world ran on this assumption that swans were supposed to be white, so nobody was ever able to predict that black swans would ever be a thing, too.*

"*So the 'black swan theory' is where you build long-term predictions while bound by your current state of comprehension, but thereby fail to account for unpredictable events even after they happen…*

"*If you've had ten years straight of bountiful harvests, you'd never imagine that a flood would ravage your farmland tomorrow, right?*"

No, you wouldn't. A strain of Varanium-immune Gastrea? Who would ever guess? And if the virus ever got out and their numbers started multiplying, the human race would immediately lose all their safe zones. Every nation, every human being would meet their maker. The Gastrea conquest of planet Earth would be complete.

This was the Black Swan Project. What an ugly, horrible, disgusting thing. And most of all, Rentaro couldn't believe this was all the work of mankind.

"But what's the Five Wings Syndicate going to do with these…?"

Rentaro shook his head. "If they had enough of these Varanium-resistant Gastrea, they could deliberately set off a pandemic anytime they liked…"

"They can't! There's no way you can domesticate Gastrea like that. They're never going to listen to them. They've already tried implanting electrodes in their minds, and it didn't work. Even if all the Gastrea in there were released right now, they'd just scatter off in a million different directions."

"The trifdraphizin."

Hotaru's eyebrows arched.

"That's the one puzzle we still haven't solved. Why is the Five Wings Syndicate so desperate for trifdraphizin that they're willing to risk blowing their cover to buy up the black-market supply? That drug puts its victims in a deep hypnotic state. Maybe they're putting the Gastrea they're raising here in a catatonic state and—I don't know how—but maybe conditioning them into attacking or going toward Tokyo Area? You know, like how they condition soldiers to immediately pull the trigger when a target appears."

Conditioning was the way people trained animals to perform certain tasks—instilling a conditioned reflex that made them perform the action on command. If you stuck a mouse in a maze and conditioned it with cheese to memorize the correct path, it would eventually run through the entire thing without hesitation—without cheese—simply because it was conditioned to run the maze. And after a soldier was conditioned in boot camp to open fire the moment he saw a target, he'd be able to pull the trigger independent of his own will, improving the chances of killing his enemy. Army commanders loved it, but it had a side effect: post-traumatic stress disorder. Making soldiers kill people they didn't want to kill. Committing these murders permanently altered their mental state, and there was no limit to the mental fallout and subsequent health bills.

All of it showed that conditioning worked, even on high-level animals like humans. Gastrea couldn't be any different.

"But... But even if it's theoretically possible, what are the chances of it working without a hitch?"

"That's why they're conducting this whole experiment. To see."

Rentaro looked up at the dome. The muscat grapes on the vines distracted him too much to notice that the dome, about two hundred meters in diameter, had a tangled mesh of pipes and wires snaking down from the center, like a tall, straight tree trunk. The dome was, in a way, a vast, computerized tree, the pipes keeping the grapevines alive.

"I'm sure Five Wings releases the Gastrea grown here all the time as an experiment. To see whether they can get into Tokyo Area or not, you know? And they put that star-and-wing mark on them so they can tell them apart from other Gastrea. Then they have crews pick them up. I'm sure the Gastrea you and Suibara killed was Varanium-resistant, too. Normally, it would've been whisked away before it ever made it to Dr. Surumi's operating table—but she found out. She knew too much. So they eliminated her."

This is what you wanted to tell me. Isn't it, Suibara?

Rentaro heard a sob behind him. He found Hotaru down on her knees, face buried in her hands.

"Why...?" she wailed, shaking her head back and forth. "Why did Kihachi have to die for this...? Just being with Kihachi made me so happy, and then...*this* happened...!"

It was true; Hotaru was just as much a victim of the Black Swan Project as the others. And she might have more company soon. If Black Swan ever got out, Tokyo Area would be crushed. Suibara tried to blow the whistle on them. He knew how dangerous it'd be for him, but he tried anyway.

If we crack under pressure now, the thing Suibara lost his life trying to reveal will be lost in the darkness again. The Five Wings Syndicate will just continue their experiments somewhere else.

Rentaro couldn't bear to let that happen. He shook his head lightly and looked up at the giant tree in front of him.

"You know what, Hotaru? I was wrong. I thought that if I came back with some evidence, that'd be enough to clear my name. But this is on a whole other level now. We can't let a single Gastrea get out of this facility. We have to kill them all right here."

"How?"

Rentaro turned his head toward the center of the cultivation room. Hallways fanned out from the large pipe in the center. They were fairly basic in structure, the floors made out of steel mesh that looked like it was recycled from the construction phase. Rentaro picked the nearest one and walked toward the trunk, his soles clanking against the metal, and Hotaru following. Looking down, he saw that the catwalk spanned above a mass of wires—the "roots" of the tree, so to speak.

White fog steamed around, dissipating into a thick, milky mist. The chill they felt must have come from the evaporating liquid nitrogen, or whatever this was. Something told him that falling on those cords could be hazardous to their health.

Upon reaching the center of the dome, he and Hotaru checked out the assorted machinery accessible to them. It seemed to control operations around the vineyard. Destroying it might kill off the Gastrea gestating inside.

It made Rentaro marvel at his enemy all over again. The Five Wings

Syndicate had the resources to build this massive facility. What kind of scale were they built on? And how far had they sunk their talons into Tokyo Area by now?

It was lucky they had stayed constantly on guard this time, expecting the enemy at any moment. It paid off when, all of a sudden, they felt a menacing presence behind their backs.

On went the cybernetic arm. The extractor installed inside grabbed a cartridge. The ejector kicked it away from his body.

Tendo Martial Arts First Style, Number 13—

"—*Rokuro Kabuto!*"

The swirling motion he added to his fist as it whizzed through the air collided against something advancing upon him from Hotaru's side. For a moment, a shock wave crossed the room, like the air itself had been deconstructed. With a loud boom, the object—a rifle round—was deflected into oblivion.

Rentaro turned in the bullet's direction. Hotaru, taking another moment or two to realize she had been targeted, swiveled her head around, searching fruitlessly.

"Welcome, Satomi. I figured you'd be coming."

A shadowy figure trudged its way across the corridor. He had a broad nose and an ice-cold stare, but above the boy's popped uniform collar, a twisted smile was painted on his face. He brought the sniper rifle lingering over the mist back to his side, stuck both hands in his pockets, and walked toward Rentaro.

"Yuga Mitsugi," muttered Rentaro, voice filled to the brim with disgust. There was no sense of surprise. Sooner or later, he knew the guy would show up. And he knew that, so long as he failed to take him down in battle, there would be no victory against the Five Wings Syndicate.

"Hotaru," Rentaro said, eyes still fixed upon Yuga, "I need you to do me a favor. Take all the plastic explosives in the bag and plant them around the main parts of the lab. I'll join you once I beat this guy."

"But I wanna—"

"*Please.* I need to settle things with him personally."

Hotaru frowned at the interruption.

"...Good luck, Rentaro. Please don't die."

With that, she mentally shook off her concerns, picked up her traveling bag, and headed for the main door. Rentaro followed her from the corner of his eye until she disappeared, then turned back to the presence in front of him.

Silence reigned for a few moments, accompanied by the mist billowing around them. Except for all the machines humming, it almost looked like they were standing on a rope bridge deep in some uncharted mountain valley.

"I've got you, Yuga Mitsugi," Rentaro rumbled in a low voice. "I know what you're doing. I'm gonna blow the whistle."

"I'm gonna have to give you a 'no' on that."

"What is Five Wings after? Are you gonna sell the Varanium-resistant Gastrea to some third-world terrorist or something?"

"Sell them? Why would we do something like that? We're gonna *use* them."

Rentaro had trouble understanding this for a moment. The logical part of his brain refused to accept it.

"Use…them?"

"Exactly." Yuga broadly extended his arms and began to breezily pace in a circle around his adversary. "The mission of the Five Wings Syndicate is world hegemony. World dominance. I don't know how it was before the war, but the Five Areas of Japan comprise one of the richest countries in the world. We're a major Varanium exporter, and we're a world leader when it comes to technology. By themselves, the rest of the world's nations are helpless. Like badgers hunkered down in their badger holes. We need to step up in their place, maintain world order, and exterminate the Gastrea on a worldwide level. But in order to achieve that, we need to bring the world under our administration. To make sure everyone's marching to the beat of the same drum. *Our* drum."

Rentaro narrowed his eyes.

"But it's tragic, though, isn't it?" Yuga continued. "All the different races, religions; all the conflicting ideologies in the world. Too many nations that would never listen to our call to action. If we want to keep everyone on the same wavelength, first we have to clear out the countries that aren't reasonable. That's what the Varanium-resistant Gastrea are for."

"Clear out...? How is that different from taking over the world?"

"It's completely different. We're trying to provide proper guidance to the world. That's what it takes to create a Gastrea-free planet. And as part of that effort, we need to step up. The US used to be called the 'world police' a long time ago—well, now it's our turn. We have to take their place and make the troublemaker nations of the world submit to us. After all, it's truly a pity, but mankind—the supposed ruler of all things in the world, that most social of animals—is simply unable to create a form of government without an elite ruling class. As supposedly intelligent as we all are, we're still so blindly obedient to authority. It's just like a colony of ants. That's why we need to teach people who the queen ant is around here. The Five Wings Syndicate, you know... It transcends borders. It transcends political affiliations. It's a group of people distressed by the destruction of their native lands, working under the same flag to make the world a better place."

"Are you being serious at all?"

"I'll tell you that, at the very least, the people above me truly think this. That's why the vanguard force of this group is the New *World* Creation Project. Not New Humanity."

With a blaze of speed, Rentaro drew his gun and fired at Yuga's feet. The bullet ripped through the sole. The barrel, as hot as his own anger, pounded against the side of his arm.

"Don't give me that shit. Is that what Suibara had to die for? *That?* You made Hotaru break down in tears for *that* bullshit?"

Yuga shrugged his shoulders in a not-my-problem gesture.

"I'm sick of all this talking. We're never *not* going to be in conflict with each other... Now I know that all too well!"

Rentaro's left eye, and both of Yuga's, activated simultaneously. The preliminary calculations were underway.

"Today's going to be a great day," Yuga hissed. "Let's get started. The New Humanity Creation Project, or the New World Creation Project—which is the truly legitimate evolution of mankind?"

The final battle between Rentaro and Yuga was underway.

It was heralded by a particularly large burst of billowing mist, hiding both figures within. It cut off Rentaro's ability to harness his cybernetic eye—but his foe was in the same boat. He pushed off the ground and, at astonishing speed, covered ten meters in a single instant. Next came Tendo Martial Arts First Style, Number 5—*Kohaku Tensei*—and despite not using a cartridge, his fist zoomed across the air at subsonic speed, blowing away the white mist. But it was Rentaro whose eyes burst open in surprise afterward. The enemy he sought was not there.

The next moment, an intense pain raced across his temple. He blacked out for half a moment.

"Ngh!"

Looking back, he saw that Yuga was somehow by his side now, about to unleash a kick. In his right hand, he gripped a large knife—really more of a short sword. The path it took for his follow-up attack seemed to leave white-hot afterimages, like a flash of lightning. The CPU in Rentaro's eye raced to gauge this threat. It found an escape route just in time. He turned his head back to dodge, wound his elbow up, tensed his arm, and aimed a knee kick to Yuga's face. It was blocked just before it made impact.

His enemy's face was right in front of him now, twisted with hate. It seemed to Rentaro like that face was sunken into his head. Then stars went off in his mind. By the time he realized he had been the victim of a head butt, he was spewing blood from his nose and taking several unbalanced steps backward. His vision lurched. The blood *plink*ed against the metal catwalk, like crimson flowers on a meadow.

When he looked back up, Rentaro had lost Yuga in the heavy mist again. He almost fell into a panic, just barely retaining his wits.

I can't track him with my eyes.

I am my gun, and my gun is me: The unity of man and machine, so expertly honed in the VR training Rentaro undertook to defeat Tina, was attuned not only to his own gun, but to the sound of the trigger bar scraping against his enemy's frame, the firing hammer going down through the sear.

Just as he dove to the right, a flash erupted from the fog. The scream of gunpowder deafened his ears.

"Wha…?!"

Somehow, despite both sides being robbed of their artificial-eye skills, Rentaro dodged the bullet. The surprise was obvious in Yuga's yelp. Rentaro was instantly there. By the time Yuga adjusted his aim, Rentaro's fist was already speeding within range. Both hands were free; both feet were planted on the ground.

"Tendo Martial Arts First Style, Number 15—"

A cartridge made an ominous *ka-chack* as it tumbled out. Rentaro's Super-Varanium fist propelled itself at unthinkable energy levels as it tore at Yuga from below. It broke the sound barrier and, like a wrecking ball, blew the mist away. In a panic, Yuga crossed both arms in self-defense. It was pointless.

"*Unebiko Ryu—!* You're outta here!"

The uppercut, curving from below toward Yuga's chin, smashed through his left arm. It sent his body a good ten meters away.

But he wasn't done. Launching a leg cartridge to thrust him forward, Rentaro closed in for a second attack. Drawing a semicircle in the air with his body, he rose up to Yuga's midair position and launched another leg cartridge. The casing arced in the air, tracing a gold-tinged path behind him.

Tendo Martial Arts Second Style, Number 16: *Inzen Kokutenfu*.

"Raaaaah!"

The flying roundhouse kick buried itself into the still-midair Yuga's stomach, this time sending his body downward. He crashed against the bare steel of the catwalk with a loud clanging sound, bouncing several times from the force of the impact before putting a dent in the anti-fall railing.

How's that?!

To a normal human, the first uppercut would have been enough to crush every bone in their body. No matter how mechanized his body was—

"Huh?!"

Rentaro found his eyes opening wide in shock once more. Yuga stirred, hoisting himself up via the dented railing. He had nothing to say, his tousled hair covering one eye. The other one, its iris spinning rapidly, glared at him.

"I'll kill you."

"…You got me at the hotel," Rentaro replied. "Now we're even."

"I can't lose to the Tendo style a second time!"

…A second time?

As he shouted, Yuga took two survival knives from his belt, gripping one in each hand as he screamed at the heavens.

Rentaro's instinct told him not to approach, so he unholstered his gun, aimed, and fired a barrage of shots. The recoil from the nine-millimeter rocked his arm.

He realized the mistake he had made when he saw Yuga twist and turn his body to dodge them. Of *course*. He was fighting a foe with eye enhancements just like his. If he kept relying only on what he could see with his eyes, the predictive AI was going to read his bullets' trajectory every time.

The sheer speed at which Yuga then rushed toward him, body kept low to the ground, was clear from the mist he kicked up around him. Rentaro aimed his Beretta again.

But Yuga interrupted him with the throw of a knife. It stuck into the Beretta, confusing his eyeball's measurements and making him accidentally pull the trigger. The muzzle flash erupted toward nothing in particular.

The remaining knife was at Yuga's hip, shining dully in the mist as it rocketed toward Rentaro. Realizing it was too late to dodge it, he lowered his body, preparing to deflect the blade with his Super-Varanium right arm.

His entire body seemed to creak at the moment of impact, his soles sliding against the steel floor. The heat generated by the friction left the smell of something burning in the air, and the sound of metal screeching against metal greeted his ears. The blade danced by in the air, mere centimeters from his nose.

By a hair's breadth, he had stopped his opponent's bull charge. Yuga's hate-twisted face was directly in front of his. He could feel his breathing.

But once again, Rentaro misjudged Yuga Mitsugi's threat. Yuga only had a knife in his right hand. In his left he held a small, round object that he brought toward Rentaro, as if offering it to him.

Rentaro groaned, like an icy hand had a grip on his heart. He recognized that object.

An HG-86 mini-grenade.

The detonation pin and lever were already off. At this range, both were squarely in the kill zone.

A suicide strike?!

Rentaro's body reacted to the fear seizing his body. With a free elbow, he knocked the grenade away. It flew off the catwalk and fell down below, then exploded with a body-wrenching shock wave.

Yuga's left hand was now free. It struck hard against Rentaro's stomach, left wide open by his uplifted elbow. Belatedly, Rentaro realized what Yuga was doing.

Oh damn. His palm strike can—

One look at Yuga's upturned lips was enough to freeze his spine.

"Vairo-orchestration! Prepare to be shattered!"

The next instant, a withering pain beyond all imagination tore through his body.

"Gyaaaaahhhh!"

His vision was jarred. The pain made it feel like his body was being blown apart.

Without even realizing what he was doing, he flailed his feet and managed to wrest himself free. His vision was still lurching back and forth, and the pain made him fall to his knees. Rentaro looked at his wound. His guts felt loose in his body, and the amount of bleeding damage was unlike anything he had seen before. He felt a blob of something distasteful well up in his esophagus, and then blood bubbled out of his mouth, along with bits of lung that had been vibrated off. It was jet-black in color, and now it stained the floor an even more ominous shade.

His eye blurred, his body screaming out in pain. It urged him not to move—but, gritting his teeth in desperation, he looked up at Yuga. He, too, was gravely wounded. It was a wonder he could still stand. And why wouldn't it be? He had taken the full brunt of not one, but two cartridge strikes. That he was alive at all was a miracle.

"We were created ten years ago to defend the world during the Gastrea War! Don't you see how pointless fighting each other is?!" Rentaro shrieked.

Yuga swept an arm horizontally in front of him. "I believe in Professor Grünewald! That's the path I've chosen!"

"I never got used to this machine body. I had to get my limbs replaced every time I grew a bit more. It was a constant barrage of pain."

"Me too."

"I thought it was gonna kill me, once or twice."

"Me too."

"It's not too late, all right?! I don't want to kill you!"

"You're making no sense!" came Yuga's reply. "Why aren't you trying to join the ruling side? We're the chosen ones! If there's any problem with us, it's only that we can't transcend entropy—we can't make a machine that doesn't break down! Sumire Muroto made you into just as devastating a killing machine as I am! We were built to create destruction and chaos. We're practically brothers! You…and I!"

"Shut up! I'm not like you at all! Dr. Muroto gave me this arm so I could connect with people!"

"That's a pack of lies!"

"You asshole…!" Rentaro shouted as he stood up, shedding droplets of blood. His lungs shuddered in pain with every breath. White mist continued to billow out from the cords and devices around him—but all he could hear now was the beating of his own heart.

Yuga lowered his stance, preparing for action as he took his unique crossed-arms defensive tactic again. Rentaro joined him, but he chose to take the Tendo Martial Arts Water and Sky Stance instead. There was nothing defensive about it. No escape for his foe.

The cybernetic parts of each young man were operating faster than they ever had before—perhaps for the last time. Sparks of light entered their vision.

The staredown made both sides hold their breath. It was a picture of concentration in its ultimate form. Once it was released, it was over. The fists of both opponents were clenched, ready to take the life of their respective foe.

What wound up breaking the tranquility was the voice of a girl from behind the door: Hotaru.

"Rentaro!"

That was the signal. Without even a second of hesitation, Rentaro stomped his foot on the floor and set off three cartridges at the same time. He closed in on Yuga at supersonic speed, faster than a jet engine. Then he burned through one on his arm, the smell of burnt gunpowder penetrating his nostrils.

His fist unleashed itself. Yuga's own was approaching his eyes.

Tendo Martial Arts First Style, Number 8: *Homura Kasen*.

Cartridge thrust clashed with ultravibration—two of the world's most advanced technologies colliding, immediately clearing all the mist out of the room with the shock waves. Their footholds collapsed under them, the main computer emitting sparks in the background.

"Haaaaaaaaaaah!"

"Grrrrrraaaaahhhh!"

Fist collided with open palm, vying for superiority. Rentaro's opponent was in such a bad mess that Rentaro had no idea how his ultravibration device still worked. But work it did. Thunder coursed across his artificial arm, cracking his Super-Varanium fist.

Releasing a guttural, beastlike roar, Rentaro activated all his remaining cartridges at the same time.

"Unnnnn-liiiiiimited...*burrrrrrrssssst*!!"

There was an unprecedented clash of energy, to a level that not even experiments with a particle accelerator could hope to achieve. Then, like nothing ever heard before, there was the sound of machinery cracking to pieces.

Rentaro felt something tugging at him, as if trying to wrench his head from his neck. He was shot backward by the destructive blast, like two magnets repelling each other. The force sent his body against the floor a few times before he finally crashed into the tree trunk of pipes in the center of the dome. He gritted his teeth hard enough to lose one or two—but Rentaro still leapt back to his feet.

Yet he couldn't find the enemy he was pursuing. He picked up his Beretta handgun, plucking the knife out from where it was stuck.

Risking a peek down into the guts of the catwalk, he realized why there was no answer to his attack. Amidst the fog produced by the evaporating hyper-chilled liquid nitrogen, he saw Yuga plastered against a pipe, his clothes frozen to it. He was motionless. Rentaro wordlessly pointed the Beretta at him. Yuga glared back, the hatred congealing over his eyesight. His eyes rejected all sympathy.

Convincing him with words would never work now.

So Rentaro instead nudged his handgun to the side and shot a bullet through the tank next to him.

Immediately, a clear, all-freezing liquid, chilled down to negative

196 degrees Celsius, descended upon Yuga's body, emitting dense, thick clouds of evaporation.

"Gaaahhh!"

Rentaro averted his eyes. If he had any mercy to give, it lay in how the massive clouds of mist kept the decisive moment from being viewed.

There was the crackling of rapidly freezing matter. Then silence.

A strong, cool breeze rustled across his hair. The world was a bloom of grayish white once more.

"Rentaro…"

Hotaru clearly had something to ask. But instead of letting her continue, Rentaro walked past her.

"It's over," he said. "Let's go."

The moment they climbed the stairs from the second-floor basement to the single aboveground story, they were each forced to put a hand over their own forehead, to protect their eyes from the burning sunlight.

They hadn't realized it, since they had spent the past several hours belowground, but it was already well into daylight outdoors. Going out the facility's back door, they found themselves on top of a small hill, in the middle of a basin dug into a conical valley.

"I guess that's how they keep the Gastrea from getting in here," Rentaro said as he shaded his eyes. In front of them was a line of tall, deep-black stone Monoliths. There was hardly any room between them to go through.

"Portable Monoliths…? Is that how they claimed the land?"

Each one was about two meters in width and 3.25 meters in height. A set of mini-Monoliths, through and through, as if manufactured for a Tokyo Area–themed mini golf course. Size made all the difference in effectiveness, so these Monoliths would likely repel Stage One creatures and not much else. Against a Stage Two, they'd act as a mild deterrent; anything tougher, and the best you could hope for was a good running start.

They were familiar enough to Rentaro. Varanium mining operations in the Unexplored Territory always deployed sets of these, usually accompanied by civsec bodyguards. Maybe that was Swordtail's and Hummingbird's day job around there.

"What'd you do with the explosives?"

"I placed them on the load-bearing columns across the building. We can set all of them off at the same time. I took a bunch of pictures of the facility, too, so we're good to go evidence-wise."

"Okay. Let's move back a bit and set it off. We'll have to watch to make sure the whole thing collapses."

"Hang on. If we blow it up now, we won't be able to take the train back."

Rentaro gently shook his head. "Their plan was probably to have Yuga ambush and kill me in the lab. We just turned the tables on them. I guess New World can monitor their assassins' vital signs somehow, so the enemy already knows he's dead by now. There's no guarantee they won't blow the tunnel while we're running that train down it. We can't afford to let up for a single moment until we hand over the evidence and bring Five Wings to public light."

Hotaru eyed the Monoliths nervously—the real ones, off in the far distance.

"Can we make it back okay?"

"The Monoliths' magnetic field reaches out five kilometers past the border. We're around sixteen kilos from there now, so once we walk eleven, we're in the clear. Even if we run into any Gastrea on the way, they're gonna be Stage One, Two at most. Strength-wise, we've got nothing to worry about. The sun's gonna set on the way, but I think we can manage."

He couldn't tell how much of the bravado in his voice made it across to Hotaru. But she seemed to accept it well enough. She looked up to him, an optimistic smile on her face.

"All right. But let's bury *those* Gastrea alive first."

Rentaro nodded lightly.

They marched past the line of mini-Monoliths, standing proudly as they sucked up the intense daylight sun, and climbed up the valley. Once they reached a position where they had a full view of the lab, Hotaru took out the wireless switch to activate the explosives and removed the plastic cover on the button. Rentaro tensed himself up with anticipation as he looked down at the lab.

"Rentaro."

Hotaru's voice had an odd sort of wistfulness to it. It seemed rather out of place. Turning to her, Rentaro found her slightly flush around the cheeks, an affable smile on her face.

"Thanks."

"Thanks for what?"

"For everything up to now."

Rentaro's eyes darted away. He scratched his head, unable to reply to this unfamiliar appreciation on Hotaru's part.

"Kind of too early to thank me, isn't it? It's gonna be hilarious if those explosives turn out to be a dud."

Hotaru brought a hand to her eyes, chuckling as she shook her head a bit. "Rentaro, I…I know maybe you don't want to hear this from me, but…"

Maybe it was an Initiator's sixth sense sounding a warning to her.

Looking at the lab, Hotaru's eyes shot wide open. She ran back up to Rentaro. Unable to comprehend this, Rentaro found himself thrown into the air. He couldn't recover in time, hitting his head against a stone on the ground as stars filled his eyes.

"…Ow!" Rentaro shouted. "What're you—?"

Rentaro managed to make it this far before he ran out of words.

"I'm glad you're…okay, Rentaro."

Hotaru dimly smiled as she stood there. She waddled forward with unsteady steps, trying her best to stay on her feet. A trail of blood ran from the edge of her lips.

Looking down, Rentaro saw that her abdominal area—the light pink in her tank top—was now stained a deep red.

This was the point at which the second sniper bullet probably came along.

It ripped Hotaru's chest area open. Warm blood spattered on Rentaro's face. She immediately lost her balance, falling to her knees, head down, before collapsing on top of Rentaro.

His eyes remained open in disbelief as he broke the shattered girl's fall.

"Hotaru?"

3

He had just shot down his target, but there was no particularly deep sense of victory.

Yuga's hand pulled back the bolt handle. It ejected the empty

cartridge and sent the next round into the chamber. It was a procedure he could conduct as naturally as his own breathing.

"…Checkmate."

The low, hushed voice was bereft of warmth, enough to make any onlooker's blood run cold. It sounded more like a groan wafting in from the underworld.

As it should be, for he would be visiting there soon.

Yuga took his attention away from the window for just a moment, staring at his own legs. Everything below the thighs was gone.

But, for two reasons, there was only a slight trickle of blood. One, Yuga's legs were already half-machine, bolstered by carbon nanotubes and enhanced artificial musculature, and there was a litany of fail-safes installed that would constrict blood vessels and shut off the flow of blood for him. Two—and this was the simpler one—by the time Yuga managed to amputate his own legs, everything from the thighs down was already frozen solid.

The shower of liquid nitrogen over his body felt so *hot* as it flowed across his nervous system. It nearly drove him insane before killing him. Just before it could, he managed to shut down his pain receptors and perform the amputation in more or less cruise-control mode. He had to hand it to himself. He was one hell of a war machine.

Now that the worst was behind him, Yuga had crawled out of the Gastrea cultivation room, lifted himself up step-by-step across the ramp, recovered his sniper rifle, and made his way to a first-floor window. It was sheer, unrelenting force of will that drove him, and nothing else.

Hotaru Kouro was no longer on his mind. She didn't register with the solidified ball of obsessive hatred within him. No part of his body wanted anything more than to dispatch his enemy. He was a physical manifestation of murderous intent.

The gunshots were like the cheering of well-wishers in his ears. The recoil was like a hand rocking his cradle. The smell of spent gunpowder was the sweet scent of a gourmet meal.

Still half-dead, he'd used his silencer to break the glass of the lab window, rested the barrel on the sill, and shot the enemy on top of the hill with his rifle—all in a single, fluid motion.

The bullets were filled with concentrated Varanium, modified to stay embedded within the victim's body.

His next shot had missed. By then Rentaro had dragged Hotaru's body behind the hill, but he had dropped the activation switch she was carrying on the slope. If he wanted it back, he would have to run back into range.

But Yuga had no reason to be optimistic. His frozen bottom half would unfreeze soon enough. The blood oozing from his legs' capillary tubes would render his mechanical blood flow–restriction abilities moot. He might die from blood loss.

No. He couldn't have that happen. Right now, Yuga was a sniper. Even if all the blood spurted out of his body, the moment Rentaro entered his line of vision, he would pull the trigger back like the perfect sniper he was. And once he saw his opponent fall dead, he would probably expire right then.

A sniper never sleeps until their target is completely dead.

Both of his cybernetic eyes rotated at high speed, making their preliminary calculations.

"It's not over! It's not over yet. Come on! Get over here, Rentaro Satomi…!"

What little warmth Hotaru had left in her arms began to ebb. Her perforated, blood-filled lungs breathed in shallow mouthfuls of the final air they'd taste, like a broken pair of bellows. It was something wholly different from the period of cataleptic regeneration she normally fell into.

Part of him asked himself why. Another grew to accept it.

There were all the omens. Why did Yuga go and fire the first shot inside the lab's vineyard at Hotaru? Swordtail must have told him all about Hotaru's regenerative abilities before he died. He knew that, but he still wasted his time on a seemingly pointless shot.

The most probable reason was that Yuga was taking an anti-Hotaru approach to the fight, and that was what the shot had been. Yuga was so intent on facing off against Rentaro that he used that first shot to get rid of any outside elements as soon as possible. That was the only valid explanation.

In other words, he had a way all along to kill her for good—

Rentaro closed his eyes and let out a heavy sigh. He knew what he had to do.

"Rentaro, am I…?"

Hotaru's eyes were open but groggy. Her lips were purple and shaky, but apart from that, it was like she had just woken up from a dream. He gripped her hand and looked straight into her eyes.

"It's nothing serious. You're gonna recover from it. You'll be fine."

Hotaru let out a relieved sigh. Apparently she was already beyond the point where she felt pain. Her expression was calm.

Slowly, she raised a shaking hand. Following her fingertip, he saw it was pointed at her M24 sniper rifle, scope mounted. He realized what she meant.

"I… No." He retreated. "I can't."

Hotaru smiled. "Please. Just do it. If you don't, the Gastrea are gonna… be sent all over Tokyo Area. If they do that…"

Hotaru, you have no idea how poorly trained I am at sniping. I really could just…never. I had my enemy one hundred meters in front of me on Tokyo Tower, and I missed twice. *Meanwhile, my enemy can head-shot a man riding a Shinkansen train from 1,200 meters away. We could hold this face-off a thousand times, and the outcome would be obvious. Every single time.*

But the girl's earnest eyes were still filled with the light of trust.

Rentaro closed his eyes, then opened them.

"All right."

Rentaro picked up the sniper rifle again, taking it by the handle and removing the safety.

"I promise I'll kill him and blow up the lab. There's nothing to worry about."

"But…"

Rentaro gently cut her off.

"This is the 'savior of Tokyo Area' you're talking to. Don't you believe me?"

Hotaru's face grew more serene. She haltingly shook her head.

"The, the next time I wake up… I think I can be nicer to you next time, Rentaro."

"Yeah."

"I think...I'll have more courage than I used to. And when I do, there's something I want to tell you."

"Uh-huh."

The tears at the far edges of Hotaru's eyes fell out in a thin line.

"I finally managed to protect my partner. Now I don't have to have that dream bother me anymore. I'm not afraid of dying any longer. It doesn't hurt anymore."

Rentaro hung his head down, shaking his head silently.

"Thank you, Rentaro," she continued. "You helped bury the loneliness for me. You taught me the meaning to my life."

She turned her eyes toward the wide-open blue sky and squinted.

Her outstretched hand soon lost its strength and fell.

She never moved again.

"Thanks, Hotaru."

There were no tears. He knew full well what had to be done.

"Thanks for believing in me. Thanks for fighting with me."

If he had the time to let his eyes get clouded with tears, he had the time to defeat his enemy. He had the dreams and hopes of far too many people on his back to do anything else.

He opened the flip-up cover as Tina's advice from a bygone day echoed in his mind:

"You can't kill another person unless your own soul dies, too."

No. You're wrong, Tina. That's how a monster does it.

The path to justice is fraught with danger. It's too easy, too sweet and tempting, to let it turn you into a monster. But I can't beat him that way.

Rentaro stood up, revealing himself on the top of the hill—easily within enemy range.

Bringing his right hand up to the front stand, he stabilized the position of his gun and placed the glass-fiber stock on his left shoulder. His eye peered into the scope.

"I'm saying you need to find a reason for yourself. One that'll make it seem worth taking another person's life."

Because I want to protect. Protect Tina, protect Kisara, protect Enju. I want to save as many people as I can. With my own two hands.

And if this is what it takes—

His heart calmed itself. All was clear and serene now.
He took a breath and gradually let it out.

His eye activated.

Rentaro's line of sight expanded as his formerly closed left eye began
to function. A richly colored, almost spicy taste ran across his mouth.
The nano-core processor began to operate at superspeed, the iris spinning in a dazzling array of geometric patterns.
"Time to end this for good...Yuga Mitsugi."

Rentaro's presence in his line of sight, of course, registered as an
image in Yuga's electronic retinas. Yet, at first, Yuga thought it was
some kind of mistake.
"Standing up...and shooting with his left eye?"
Unlike firing from a kneeling or prone position, remaining on your
feet made it extremely difficult to keep the gun steady, boosting the
difficulty of landing a hit from far away to astronomical levels. If hand
shake resulted in even a millimeter's worth of difference, there would
be no way to recover from as little as two hundred meters out. And
since he was using his artificial eye to aim, that meant he had to be
using his left hand to pull the trigger—his nondominant hand.
It looked like suicide to Yuga—from a common-sense standpoint,
that was. But then, the war pyre in his mind burned brighter than ever.
Rentaro was there, on the same stage as he was. It made his chest burn.
*All right, then. What I have to do doesn't change. One shot is all it
takes.*
His eyes revved up even faster, throwing off an intense heat. It was
Yuga's first experience with "overclocking" his own hardware. Time
passed slowly as both of his eye sockets burned. The eyes completed
their ballistics and landform calculations. He rested his finger on the
trigger of his DSR rifle.
Not lagging behind a single moment, his opponent fired simultaneously.
There was a crack. The recoil kicked against his shoulder.

Then came the shrill sound of glass breaking. The figure in the scope fell to his knees and disappeared behind the hill.

Yuga didn't remove his eye from the scope. But he could tell that Rentaro's bullet had gone through the window next to his. He had gauged it wrong. He operated the handle and loaded the next round.

It was a hit. But he still twisted his body a moment before. It wasn't lethal.

"Nhh...graaahh!"

Rentaro dropped his rifle. It kicked up some dust as he fell to his knees.

The sniper bullet had dug into the side of his stomach, delivering a second blow to the Vairo-orchestration wound. Blood seeped between the fingers of both hands as he tried to block the wound, now dripping into the grass. The greasy sweat running down his face disappeared into the dry earth.

Half-crazed from the pain, he pulled his jaw back and thrust his forehead against the ground. Then another time, then another. The skin on his forehead broke open, spitting blood.

His breathing was raw and animal-like in the gaps between his gritted teeth. Spittle flew out of his mouth.

Just stay down. Next time you bring your face up, it's gonna be gone.

Shut up. I have to do this. For Hotaru. For Suibara. For everyone who's had to die so far.

Rentaro's sixth sense told him Yuga's eyes were heating up. He could feel his own speed toward oblivion as well. It was like coevolution—two animals affected by each other as they evolved over time.

100x, 200x, 300x—it kept ratcheting up. He felt like his eye was catching on fire.

He raised his head and gently shook it. The world was bending around him, like a video dropping frames. Time seemed to go faster and faster.

The air grew viscous, the sun losing its shine and going ever further toward darkness. It felt like being dragged alive to the bottom of the sea; the sound around him grew low, heavy, and monotone, losing all meaning.

Rentaro crawled forward to keep from falling into range, scrambling to pick up his sniper rifle again. He operated the handle, ejected the cartridge, and loaded in the next one.

Still on his knees, he steadied the gun barrel on the hill and looked into the scope. He aimed.

The enemy was quicker this time, too. He had a hunch, and nothing but a hunch. But that was why he pulled the trigger and rolled.

A sniper shot ripped through Rentaro's former location. The dirt it kicked up hit him in the face. He readied himself again, face covered in dirt and mud, and gritted his teeth while he peered into the scope.

This time, he could *not* fall back. He could *not* get scared. The speed of his thoughts now extended past 1500x. Still faster, faster. His body felt so much slower in comparison, desperately trying to respond to his thoughts. It frustrated him.

Now past 1900x. His eyeball felt like it would scream, or evaporate into thin air at any moment. Sparks ran across it as it wore itself out.

—Then Rentaro's world went into whiteout. Sound, life; all the pressures upon him vanished.

For a moment, before he realized what had happened, he thought he'd been hit and died. But that wasn't it. He was definitely conscious. The effects of the adrenaline made it so that he was temporarily numb, but the gunshot wound in his stomach was definitely still there.

He brought his left hand up to his face, opening and closing his fist a few times. He looked around. It was a bright, pure shade of white. The battle simulator in the Shiba Heavy Weapons basement was like this—an otherworldly shade of white.

But this wasn't the VR room. *Wait. This is*—

"...The terminal horizon?"

"There's a limiter circuit in your eye that ensures its processing speed doesn't go above a certain level."
Sumire's cynical voice echoed in his memory.
"...you'd see too much. It probably feels like time's slowing down for you as your eye calculates the enemy's range and future position, but it

can still go a lot further than that. We transplanted a version of your eye without a limiter into several patients, but none of them ever came back.

"...a second of real time slows down to what feels like two thousand to you. That's the terminal horizon. All the patients who crossed that never came back. Their brains were completely fried."

So this was the "horizon" all those patients saw, then? *Or am I looking through the eyes of God at the moment?*

Those trivialities didn't matter. His enemy was seeking him.

A figure bathed in light appeared about ten meters in front of him. It gradually formed itself into Yuga. He was in sniper position at a hill in the middle of a conical valley, so he should have had his gun pointed downward—but there he was, staring right at him. They were over two hundred meters away from each other, but now he was so close, he could see the expression on his face.

Yuga was glaring at him, dour and concentrated. But Rentaro had the impression that his focus wasn't quite on where he was kneeling.

But that didn't matter. He planted the M24 against his shoulder. Yuga, a beat later, took his own stance.

He squeezed the trigger.

I won.

Just as he thought that, he heard the roar of a collision like never before. Sparks flew into his line of sight.

It was a scene no regular person could have ever comprehended. But Yuga, with his overclocked eyes feeding information to his overclocked brain, could.

"No..."

With a sonic boom, two faster-than-sound shots surged through the air. Their positions were millimeter-perfect. They collided in front of his face, sending the shot he knew was destined to kill Rentaro away from its target.

"Bullet to bullet...?"

This was nothing anyone could do on purpose. The entire philosophy Yuga brought to his sniper duties screamed it to him: No one could trigger this on purpose.

His eyes remained wide open in shock. But his hands kept going, moving like they were a different creature. Release the empty cartridge. Load in a new round. Take aim. Apply ballistics correction with his eyes, and fire.

Another sharp sound. His opponent didn't fall, and neither did he. All that remained was the echoing sound of the gunshots.

Yuga's entire body shook. It…it *wasn't* a coincidence. He was pulling off the superhuman feat of stopping his bullets in midair with his own gunshots. *How could that possibly ever* work? *I have two cybernetic eyes. The Professor told me himself—I am the most gifted user of these eyes the world has ever known.*

"…That's bullshit. That's *bullshit!!*"

Compared to the enraged Yuga, Rentaro was in a state of transcendent bliss.

If both sides' abilities granted them perfect accuracy with each shot, the common-sense rules of sniper combat—shoot, then run away—no longer applied. There was no longer any reason to use them.

The moment Rentaro pulled the trigger, his breathing didn't even stop. He was firing without bothering to adjust for the difference in height and zeroing range between them. But he was hitting.

His eye, directly connected to his mind, took over full control of his muscular system, including the motor area of his brain. Rentaro's entire body was transformed into a self-sufficient sniper system.

Yuga had aimed at him several times. His opponent hadn't even pulled the trigger yet, but Rentaro could already see the bullet's arc in the air.

Rentaro tilted his head slightly to dodge the projected trajectory, then fired. A rough, curt blast erupted from his muzzle, the bullet crashing through the rifling and into the air at supersonic speed. Yuga's bullet whizzed near his ear, scraping him.

The sonic boom cut by Rentaro's cheek. Blood flew.

He twisted the handle back to eject the cartridge. The empty shell flew through the air as he loaded another Lapua Magnum round.

Yuga, through Rentaro's scope, held his mouth open, eyes like saucers. He could see his tongue fly up to the roof of his mouth to form the *Nnn* sound, then his lips rounding themselves into an O.

It's over, Yuga Mitsugi.

He pulled the trigger. The firing pin struck the bottom of the cartridge through the sear and bolt. The sound of a gunshot. The kick of the rifle against his shoulder.

Yuga made no response to the death-dealing bolt coming his way. Right up to the bitter end, his face belied his attempt to deny everything in his mind.

4

Crushing pebbles under the soles of his shoes, Rentaro came in from behind the pile of chalk construction material. The facility was silent.

Opening the door, Rentaro cut across the C-shaped corridor and walked straight ahead. After a while, he stopped. "Yo."

"Hey."

Yuga lay flat against the floor, arms and leg stubs splayed across it. His DSR sniper rifle had slid across the room, abandoning its master for the last time.

"How did the battle turn out? Why...? Why did I...?"

He used his barely functioning head to look at the blasted-open mess that was his torso. "Ahh...," he groaned, a mix of astonishment and resignation apparent in his breath.

Rentaro had trouble figuring out what to say. This was the man who killed Hotaru. He should have been cursing him. All the hate in the world wasn't enough for him.

But at the same time, he couldn't shake the feeling that he was that man. Lying down there was a cybernetic-eye user, someone who had to undergo torturous limb upgrades at regular intervals. Someone shunned by his peers.

"If we didn't have to meet like this, maybe we coulda been friends, huh?"

Yuga closed his eyes, in a comfortable state of repose. "That's a pretty pointless what-if... But I wouldn't have minded it."

"Were you in that white space, too?"

"White space...? No. What are you talking about?"

"...Never mind."

"Both of my eyes," Yuga continued, guessing at the portent of

Rentaro's question, "made it up to 1800x. I heard that my eyes could use all my emotions as fuel. They'd rev up and go down, depending. Anger, sadness, hatred, cursing, hope, happiness… But I guess my hatred and feelings of inferiority weren't enough to outclass your emotions. What did you use to go faster than me?"

"I cared about other people."

"Well…that's out of my ballpark," Yuga chuckled derisively to himself, whispering the words into the air. "No wonder I couldn't beat you. That last shot… I couldn't even see your hands between ejection and reloading. That's how fast it was."

"…So that's how your eyes saw it."

Rentaro decided to change the subject.

"Yuga, what's the Five Wings Syndicate?"

"It's an international, cross-political movement. We're everywhere. There's no guarantee the people you trust aren't part of it, either…heh-heh."

"…You mentioned how the wings around the pentagram on your arm indicated your rank. You had four of those wings, and they took two away from you. What'd you do?"

Yuga emptily chuckled again. "Nothing," he wheezed. "Like I told you, I was Professor Grünewald's favorite son up to that point. I got to work by his side. But there was a single confrontation—a single one—and I lost it. They took the wings away, and I was no longer the Professor's favorite."

"You lost it? You?"

"Yes. To another Tendo user."

"Wha…?"

"Remember? 'I can't lose to the Tendo style…again'? I wanted to beat you because…well, okay, there was probably some personal emotion there."

"…What kind of Tendo skill? Sword drawing? Aikido? Divinity? There're a lot of different types."

"The same as yours."

"Martial Arts? You're kidding me…"

Had anyone else taken on the successor role? He couldn't think of anyone.

"It took just twelve seconds," Yuga said with an ironic smile. "I don't even know how he got close to me. I looked up, and there he was, in point-blank range. Within the first three seconds, he knocked my artificial right arm off and broke my leg. It was all him from that point forward. His martial arts were a lot like yours, too…or not. His were a lot more…sinister."

"What's his name?" Rentaro confronted Yuga on the floor. "I need to know his name! Who was the guy that defeated you?"

Then he noticed the sweat glistening on his forehead. His body must have been near its limit. And Yuga had more pressing business than to answer his question.

"Satomi," he began, "have you ever seen a line of the dead?"

"Huh?"

"Before, before the Professor performed the, mechanization work on me… I told you, I was blind, right? But even though I couldn't see, I could, this one time…I saw…it. Right after, the war, the people… who were turned into, into Gastrea… They were listed as, as missing, remember? I saw it. Even through my eyelids. They weren't alive, or… or dead. A line of people, wandering through purgatory. Satomi… Heaven is so, so far away, but hell… I think, I think if I threw a stone right now, I'd hit…it."

His lips curled upward in a final self-chiding smile.

"This… This is war. Ours, and yours. The Gastrea War is… It's not, not over at…"

That was all. Yuga spat out a mouthful of blood, and softly opened his eyes, as if it was his duty to do so. He stopped moving. It was the moment Five Wings Syndicate assassin Dark Stalker left the world of the living—and with him came Yuga Mitsugi, the man who may just have been Rentaro's friend.

5

"Fuck! *Fuck!*"

Hitsuma slammed the pedal to the metal, cursing to himself every kilometer of the way. It was all over. Everything. He—Rentaro Satomi—had ruined it all.

Not long ago, Dark Stalker's vital signs had flatlined. It was clear now. Not even he could have taken on Rentaro. Dark Stalker—the man who swaggered his way into every fight he ever had, then sauntered his way back out without so much as breaking a sweat. The idea of him being shot seemed like some kind of tasteless joke.

He couldn't help but look back at all the oversights, all the possible fail-safes he ignored. Throwing him in a cell and turning his fate over to the judge seemed like the best option at the time. Now, though, it was clear that wasn't enough. If only he had poisoned the boy's meals inside jail—even if his comrades thought that was overstepping his bounds—this entire disaster could've been avoided.

Now Hitsuma had just received word from Nest to stand by and await further instructions from Five Wings. If he was stripped of his wings and expelled from the syndicate—that was the best fate he could hope for, really. But inside, he felt he had to brace himself for the idea that someone could put a bullet in his head at any moment without warning.

But even now, there was one sort of revenge Hitsuma could still exact against Rentaro. He was in a tuxedo, pushing his convertible as fast as it could go down the expressway. Eventually settling down at an intersection in a quiet suburban district, he could see the roof of the ceremonial hall, a citywide hotspot for marriages and receptions.

Despite the breakneck pace of the arrangements, he still managed to get the date he asked for. It was going to be a Western-style ceremony, and yet his fiancée's family insisted upon holding it on the most auspicious day possible in the old-style Japanese lunar calendar. He was highly dubious at first, but it was a Tendo tradition—and he still had the clarity of mind to keep at least one ear open to their requests.

In just a bit more time, Hitsuma would be married. Married to a girl Rentaro had feelings for. The wild beast that lurked in Hitsuma's psyche sneered in abject derision.

I'm going to *defile* her. *Trample* over her. Just imagining the rage with which he planned to go at her seemed to charge something up in his heart of hearts.

Checking his watch, he cursed himself once more. He needed to hurry. He was already a few minutes late. His foot was heavy on the accelerator again.

Leaving his convertible to the valet, he strode into the pompously magnificent church edifice, looking up at the cross at its very apex as he opened both front doors with both hands. The air felt secluded, a little stuffy, the only light from burning candles. They lined the walls atop metal stands; but after racing around in broad daylight, it seemed intensely dark to Hitsuma.

The space was lined with stone columns, two side aisles intersecting the main one in the middle to form another cross. Down the middle was a red carpet, and beyond it, above the altar, deep azure light streamed in through a stained-glass window. And at the altar itself—

"Oooh…!"

Hitsuma stared in astonishment. The tens of millions of yen he spent flattering her was now completely forgotten. There she was, the veil covering her black silken hair, the white gloves on her hands. The soft chiffon skirt draped over her sides. She was a maiden of pure white, one more beautiful than anyone thought possible, and she was standing with her back turned to him.

The priest had yet to arrive, it seemed, so instead of awaiting further instructions, he forgot himself and walked forward, past the long wooden pews. Once he was close enough, he reached out with a hand, aiming for her slender shoulder.

"I'm so glad you're here, Kisara. Are you ready? Once the priest shows up, we can hold the ceremony all by ourselves."

His hand touched her shoulder.

—Only to be slapped back. A long, metallic black tube zeroed in on the bridge of Hitsuma's nose. The black-haired bride narrowed her gaze at him.

"Sorry, but I'm not marrying you, Mr. Hitsuma… Or maybe it's better to call you Atsuro Hitsuma, top manager at the Five Wings Syndicate?"

"Wha…?! Kisara, what are you talking about? The Five Wings… what? I have no idea what that is—"

"—Maybe you've kept the game going for this long, Superintendent," said another voice in the distance, "but it's just about time to pay the piper."

Hitsuma whirled around. Near one of the side aisles, the door to the priest's office opened. Out of it stepped a barrel-chested inspector. Even the old-fashioned revolver he was carrying seemed like some kind of joke.

"Inspector Tadashima…"

"Sorry, sir, but you're not gonna see any priest here today. I'm taking over for him. And instead of some Western-style wedding vows, I'm gonna be advising you, USA-style, of your Miranda rights. Hope you know a good lawyer."

"Wh-what are you two people talking about? I mean, what kind of evidence could you possibly—?"

"We've got plenty of evidence."

Kisara lifted up her left arm, the long silken glove still on it. She took a chip out from inside.

"The memory card… Where did you…?!"

The stammered reaction amounted to a de facto confession. Hitsuma didn't even care anymore. All he could do was stand there, hyperventilating.

"It was in here," Kisara said as she took out a pocket watch. The light reflected off it in a dazzling array of colors. It was the very one Hitsuma had given her during their marriage negotiations.

"You, you're *kidding* me! There's no way it could be in there. I took the whole thing apart!"

"Yeah," Kisara replied as she rapped a knuckle on the watch face, "it *was* pretty tough to spot. This watch has a pretty unique mechanism inside of it. I tried messing with it, too, but even I couldn't figure it out until the appointed hour came along."

"The appointed hour…?"

"Kihachi Suibara was supposed to give this watch to Hotaru Kouro for her birthday. That's today, by the way—August 22. And when the clock struck midnight, the mechanism played a music-box melody and sprang into action. And guess what we found inside?"

"Superintendent Hitsuma, sir," Tadashima continued, police notebook in hand, "I decided to go over everything we know about Rentaro Satomi from the ground up. The suspect testified in interrogation several times that Suibara claimed someone stole his evidence, so he wanted to be referred to Lady Seitenshi to inform her of his story directly. I checked on that, and I found three 1-1-0 emergency calls from Kihachi, summoning the police to his home. The place had been ransacked every time, to the point that the answering officers couldn't determine if it was robbery or simple vandalism.

"Looking back, it was probably meant more as a warning, wasn't it? A warning not to wade further in if you want to keep breathing. So, not to persecute our own force about this, but all they did was take down a statement and leave each time. I know we're all busy on the force, but it's a bad habit we all have—as long as nobody's bleeding, we're not exactly proactive with property crimes. It must've been during one of those break-ins that Hotaru's birthday present was stolen."

The salvos of evidence fired at Hitsuma made it hard for him to breathe at all.

"So... The card...?"

"Yep," Kisara said. "We looked at it all. I'm pretty sure the police are checking in on the Five Wings officers under you right now. Sure weren't expecting the police commissioner himself to be in on it, though."

The barrel of the revolver in Tadashima's hand was quivering with rage. He was practically crushing the handle with his death grip.

"That, and we know all about the so-called 'Black Swan Project,' too. At first, sir, I was just shocked—but now... Now, I have nothing but anger for you. I can't believe you even *considered* transforming Gastrea into biological weapons...!"

Kisara whisked her head back and forth. "Why...? Why, Mr. Hitsuma? When we met five years ago, you were the most honest, ethical person I had ever met. When did *this* happen to you?"

Everything had fallen to pieces. When it finally dawned on him, he found it extremely odd that his instinctive reaction was neither anger nor resignation to his fate.

"Well, this saves me the trouble of inviting you."

"*Inviting* me?"

Hitsuma, cool and collected, spread his arms out wide and took a step forward. Tadashima's gun shook again. A look of trepidation crossed Kisara's face.

"Did you think I joined the Five Wings Syndicate because my father

made me? Well, sadly, I didn't. I joined out of my own free will. I don't know if it's in the memory card Suibara took or not, but the aim of the Syndicate is to rid the world of Gastrea for good."

"But the way you're trying to do that is absolutely evil!"

"Why is that? We are talking about a group with a united will. A will, and a drive to press that will forward. It's the simplest thing in the world."

"And can't you hear the screams of the weak you're trampling over with your 'united will'?"

Hitsuma shrugged it off, opening his arms to Kisara again. "Oh, so you're treating me like a subhuman now?" he proclaimed. "That's a little mean, isn't it? The Five Wings Syndicate investigated the whole affair with Kazumitsu Tendo. And you, too—maybe you're denying it, but deep down in your heart, doesn't our ideology resonate with you? Or is the monster you're keeping inside your heart see an even more sinister path for the future of mankind?"

Kisara shuddered, the color draining from her face.

"That's enough, Superintendent!"

"Maybe it seems like the Varanium supply's gonna last forever to you," Hitsuma continued, ignoring Tadashima's intimidation. "But it's not. Someday, it's all gonna dry out. You've probably seen pundits go on about it in the news a hundred times by now. And Varanium is used for more than just the Monoliths. Civsecs use it for their weapons and ammo, too. Whoever controls the Varanium controls the planet—and that's not an exaggeration, either.

"Even if we collected together all the estimated Varanium ore deposits in the world, there's nowhere near enough to protect every nation. And who do you think's going to be trampled over first? It's the weak! The weak you think you're defending against us! But the sooner we can take action *now*, the more human lives we can save. In fact, if the human race keeps going the way it is now—an endless quagmire of war, consumption, wasted resources—it's entirely possible that the Gastrea will wipe us out.

"You're an intelligent woman—I know you've got it in you to understand. What we need right now is to take the first step, secure victory, and keep the war as short as humanly possible. It'll all contribute to the public good, in the end. Kisara... You have what it takes to join us."

Kisara's eyes opened wide with surprise.

"President Tendo! Don't listen to him!"

Hitsuma took out the automatic handgun he had on his person and fired.

A spurt of blood flew out from Tadashima's shirt, and horrified surprise crossed his face.

Quickly turning around, Hitsuma switched to flight mode, running down the aisle. Gunfire erupted behind him, bullets digging into the floor near his feet. He used a shoulder to bash the front door open and flew out. The bright blue sky made him wince for a moment, but soon he was inside a back alley, kicking up rain puddles as he ran with all his soul.

The whole plan was a failure. He needed to come up with a new one. For now, the first priority was lying low and reformulating his strategy. Once things settled down a bit, he could contact Kisara again and try enticing her a little more. There was no need to panic. In fact, he was cooking up a few ingenious ideas already.

Then a car burst into the alley in front of him, brakes screeching. It stopped right in the middle of the street—it was after him.

The smoked-glass window whirred down, revealing the face of a young man wearing a hunting cap.

"Hello there, Mr. Hitsuma."

Hitsuma watched him, again overcome by surprise.

"Are you...Nest?"

It was the first time they had met in person. He was, after all, just a contact agent. The man who referred Hummingbird, Swordtail, and Dark Stalker to Hitsuma, as well as handled material transport for him.

Regaining his bearings, Hitsuma started waving his arms side to side.

"The op's a failure! I need to at least get my father and myself to Osaka Area, all right? We're both gonna need fake passports, like, *now*!"

The urgency was clear in Hitsuma's voice. Nest kept on smiling.

"That's a nice bow tie you got on."

"Uh?" Hitsuma's jaw dropped as he looked down at his chest. It was a plain black one, like on every other tux in this city.

This wasn't funny. "What are you…?!"

There was a muffled gunshot, and Hitsuma's body shook.

He fell to his knees. His chest was warm. The burst of color running through his shirt was a dark red.

Nest had a pistol with a silencer attached.

"We decided to dismantle the Black Swan Project. As a result, we're being asked to eliminate all evidence linking it to Five Wings."

"No… If I'm not around, the administration's going to fall apart—"

An orange flash burst from the silencer. It was the last thing Hitsuma ever saw.

Once he fired all the bullets in his gun, Nest tossed it in the backseat and grabbed the steering wheel with both hands.

"You make a mistake, you pay for it. Farewell, my good Superintendent."

The engine revved to life as the car reversed at full speed. Another second, and Nest was gone.

All that remained was the corpse sprawled out in the wet, dingy alley.

6

Half-dead, half-alive, Rentaro wasn't able to gaze at the Monoliths in their full, up-close size until fairly well into the following night. His gait was halting, unsteady, every step met with searing pain.

It had been a long while since his battle with Yuga met its end, the blessed adrenaline his body produced in response to it a thing of the past. All that remained was an intense, all-encompassing ache.

Along the way, he encountered three Stage One Gastrea. He discovered all three first, using his few remaining leg cartridges to end the battles in half a second. And that was that.

The summer wind blew pleasantly against his skin, pallid with blood loss. He closed his eyes and sucked as much of its scent into his nostrils as possible.

He had seen it for himself—the Gastrea cultivation facility collapsing

in a heap of rubble. He had tried his best to hurry back to the Monoliths, but was stymied by the urge to carry Hotaru's body back. It made
him turn back at least once. But it just wasn't possible. Not in his state.

So he buried her next to the portable Monoliths instead. If possible,
he wanted to get her body out of that grave as soon as possible. To
someplace more suitable for her—next to Suibara.

For now, at least, the Monoliths loomed large before him.

Just beyond the border between "here" and "there," he spotted a
herd of red flashing lights. He squinted. He had no idea how they had
sniffed him out, but it looked like Rentaro had a police welcoming
party waiting for him.

He let out a sigh. The photos from inside the facility were saved on
Hotaru's mobile phone, yes. But explaining it all would take so much
more time.

But Rentaro's outlook was completely mistaken.

"Rentaro!"

"Big Brother!"

A blonde girl and another one with a pair of pigtails were running
toward him. He gazed at them in wonderment, his limbs quaking. It
had been a dream of his for so long, he seriously thought it was all a
hallucination for a moment. But when he realized it wasn't, Rentaro
started running, forgetting all about his injuries.

They half hugged, half collided into one another, spinning around
as they fell on the grass. They were warm; they were soft; they were
dreamlike—they were Enju and Tina.

"Enju! Tina!"

He tried to stop them, but he couldn't. His face twisted, and before
he knew it, the tears were surging out.

They joined shoulders, beholding one another. Tina and Enju were
just as moved by this reunion, both sniffling a little and Tina wiping her eyes at regular intervals. They repeated one another's names
over and over again like crazed parrots. One more time, they held
one another close. Strongly. Just to make sure they never separated
again.

Then, all at once, Rentaro asked a barrage of questions. Were they
free? The answer, excitedly given between the two: Yes. Enju was

suddenly released from the Promoter matching process, Tina just as suddenly released from jail, and the police even gave them a ride there.

Another question sprang to his mind. "Speaking of which, guys, we're pretty much right by the Monoliths. Are you guys okay being here, with the Gastrea Virus and all?"

"Oh," Enju replied quizzically. Then her eyebrows shot up, both hands to her mouth as her ponytails seemed to visibly droop.

"*Ngh*, I—I don't feel too good... I think I'm gonna throw up."

"I'm not too hot myself."

"Stupid."

Rentaro grinned wryly to himself as he tousled their hair. They had even forgotten about *that* for his sake.

"Come on," he said, giving both a shove on the back. "Let's get home. 'Cause, seriously, if you hang out here much longer, you'll—"

He lost his train of thought when he saw what was ahead of him. It was an August bride in white. The veil was gone, revealing a head of long, straight, black hair that waved in the wind.

"Kisara..."

She didn't try to meet his gaze. Instead she just stood there, eyes focused on a point somewhere to his right.

"Open up."

"Huh?"

"Open up your arms."

"Oh."

Rentaro did so. Kisara, still focused on the ground, fell into them, embracing his chest. Her gloved hands wrapped themselves behind his back. It unnerved him slightly.

"Wh-whoa, Kisara—"

"You're so stupid."

He couldn't gauge her expression, given that her face was buried in his torso. She rubbed her nose against it as she shook her head. A slight, ever-so-slight, shudder crossed over from her body to his.

"So, um...?" he asked.

"Yes?"

"Is it all over now?"

Rentaro felt the girl nodding in his arms. He looked up at the starless night sky and sighed.

"Oh."

Kisara was there. Enju and Tina were released. The crimes he stood accused of had all been dismissed by Kisara, apparently.

But what about her and Hitsuma? Why was she in a wedding dress? Rentaro thought for a moment, then wisely decided those questions could wait.

They stayed in that position for a while—it was hard to say how long—until Rentaro grabbed her hands and suggested they return home.

The Monoliths were right in front of them as they held each other's hands. He had been gone for so long that they were both eager to make up for lost time.

Thus the four crossed the imaginary finish line together, walking back to Tokyo Area as a group of free people.

The police officers watched blankly from their cars. After the wild goose chase Rentaro sent them on, there he was—a successful escapee, a civsec who just restored his good name right in front of them. Nobody would be getting police commendations for *this* case.

Rentaro found Tadashima's face among the watchers. He had a sling on—reportedly he had suffered a gunshot wound to the shoulder. Something about his face was even more formal and solemn than usual. He gave Rentaro a silent salute.

"Clear the way, people! The savior of Tokyo Area's coming through!"

A quiet frenzy erupted among the officers, infecting them one by one until all saluted the civsec team. Every face held a sincere look of reverence.

Suddenly, Rentaro heard the sound of a music box playing—it was from the pocket watch in Kisara's hand. There was something oddly familiar about it, but he couldn't remember the tune's name.

Despite the lack of ticker tape and cheering, it was the best welcome-home parade he could have asked for.

Thus, with the smell of summer still in the chilly wind, the police-escorted official ceremony for the reopening of the Tendo Civil Security Agency came to a close.

BLACK BULLET 6

Epilogue

SOULS UNITED, SOULS DIVIDED

Rentaro turned the handle on the faucet, filling the wooden bucket with water. He was surprised at how cold the droplets splashing out of the bucket were.

He turned his head ninety degrees upward. The sun was at its highest point in the sky. A passing airplane roared above, engines drawing a straight line across the blue.

The cemetery he stood in was located fairly close to the Outer Districts. It was surrounded by forested land, making for a loud chorus of cicadas that was less than restful. It sounded like the forest itself was yelling at them, in fact.

Holding the heavy bucket in one hand, he walked along the vast area of graves, divided into neat squares like a *go* board. Before long, he was by one of the small plots, three women behind him. They must have sensed the solemnity of the situation, for not only Tina and Kisara, but even Enju, whose energy was the defining feature of her personality, was refraining from bouncing off the walls for the time being.

The representatives of the Tendo Civil Security Agency stood before a set of gravestones, filled the water basins on them, and added bunches of flowers—bellflowers and other purple-colored varieties chief among them.

Each one took a ladle to the water, splashed it over the stones, and prayed.

"Sorry we're late in coming," Rentaro said, eyes fixed on the two stones in front of him. "Suibara... Hotaru."

Not much more needed to be said. This was the end of what was already turning out to be a fairly long conclusion.

The news was still covering Rentaro's story. In the end, an investigation exposed some thirty members of the police department, including the commissioner, involved in the conspiracy to frame Rentaro for Kihachi Suibara's murder. The cops were still poking around the wasps' nest, so to speak, looking into each co-conspirator's history to see what else they could charge them with.

Nearly all faced disciplinary measures. Most had court dates. What happened after that was for a judge to decide.

And, of course, the news didn't speak a word about the experimentation on Varanium-resistant Gastrea Rentaro had discovered. Nor anything about the Five Wings Syndicate attempting to cultivate them.

Losing Yuga and Hitsuma was a setback for Five Wings, no doubt about that, but it was far from a permanent resolution. They had already cleared the lab of any research data before Rentaro showed up, and besides, most of the conspirators they arrested were pretty low-ranking members of the force or affiliated groups. Hitsuma and his father would have known the juicy details—and both were dead, killed under mysterious circumstances. Rentaro had nothing left to pursue.

Not long after, Rentaro had paid a visit to Tamaki, Yuzuki, and Asaka at the hospital where they were recuperating. It had been something of a shock when he opened the door to their room and found Asaka and Tamaki kowtowing to him on the floor in apology. Both had broken bones, he had heard, and yet there was Asaka providing a textbook example of groveling as it was practiced in the courts of ancient China. Tamaki, on the other hand, had put his ass far too high in the air, presenting another suggestion entirely.

"We are deeply regretful that we let ourselves fall for the malicious designs of that evil force."

"A man never makes excuses. Come on, Rentaro. Just shut up and punch me in the face!"

Yuzuki, meanwhile, rested her body against one of the room's walls, seething. "Didn't I tell you?" she said. "Didn't I tell you that police officer was acting funny? I mean, like...*really*?"

This was how Rentaro had found himself in one of the most awkward moments of the year so far without so much as opening his mouth. He had to laugh at the ridiculousness of it all.

As he laughed, he'd nervously rubbed the surface of his cybernetic left eye. He hadn't seen the "terminal horizon" since his battle against Yuga—not much need to accelerate past 2000x in daily life—but his competency with a sniper rifle did improve noticeably afterward.

If anything had really changed with him, it was in the attitude he brought to his job. He now felt a certain responsibility for the deaths he had caused, directly or not. He was ready to deal with that. But that was about it.

"We should offer this, too..."

Kisara gingerly placed her pocket watch on the space between the two graves. The sentence YOU ARE ALWAYS IN MY HEART had been stamped under the cover. Suibara probably hadn't meant it when he had that stamped on, but now it felt like proof that he expected to die at any moment. It made Kisara's heart tighten a little, thinking about it.

Suibara and Hotaru risked their lives to keep Tokyo Area safe. And keep it safe they did. If it wasn't for their courageous deeds, crushing the Five Wings Syndicate's ambitions would have been impossible.

Rentaro lightly shook his head, clearing his mind.

"Let's go home."

Kisara grumbled about the fairly paltry reparations the police were willing to offer for this miscarriage of justice. Enju sprang around, attempting to burn off some energy she had built up waiting around at the IISO facility. Tina, for her part, must not have had a fun time in jail—she clammed up whenever she was asked about it, eyebrows pinned down on her face.

It was so hot, Rentaro asked Enju to buy something at a nearby vending machine, which he rarely did. Enju, always ready to annoy Rentaro one way or another, came back with a piping-hot cup of coffee. He pulled the tab and attempted a mouthful. It was hot enough to burn his tongue. From the pit of his stomach, he cursed his life.

When they arrived back at the Tendo Civil Security office—now running extended hours for summer break—Kisara arched an eyebrow. "Hey, is that car...?" she murmured, as she pointed at a well-polished black limousine parked in front of the Happy Building.

Whoever was inside must have noticed Rentaro, because the back door flew open, revealing a young woman who almost threw herself at him.

"Satomi!"

The Seitenshi was in a blindingly pure white dress. She was also wearing white heels—not exactly running gear. One heel slipped, causing her to lose her balance. Rentaro ran up and caught her just before she hit the pavement.

"Jeez, Lady—"

Rentaro's complaint was cut off when he noticed the Seitenshi's moistened eyes. They took him aback enough that he abandoned his feigned offense entirely.

"Thank you so much, Satomi. It looked like you were out of the office, so I waited here in my vehicle."

Rentaro scratched his head distractedly, averting his eyes. "No, that's...that's fine, but what brings you here in such a hurry?"

"Ah, yes," the Seitenshi said, bringing her hands together in front of her chest and taking something out of her purse. "I am here today so I can give this back to you."

"Give back...?" Rentaro said as he accepted it. He took a glance, only to find his ID photo peeking from the window of a leather card-carrying case. There was no mistaking his civsec license. He had forgotten about the Seitenshi stripping it from him at the palace, however long ago.

The gesture was so moving that he froze, license clutched in hand. Funny how he'd never thought about it much when he first got it, but now that it was back in his pocket, it made his chest feel warm and intensely grateful. He tried to say something then stopped, realizing he was about to lie. Instead, he closed his eyes and exhaled out his nose. It was almost enough to make him forget about the

Seitenshi—but, noticing her smiling right at him, he panicked a bit and turned to her.

"You, you could've just mailed it to me," he stammered. "Like, did you leave the palace just for something like *this*?"

"No... Not, not just for that, no..." The Seitenshi was stammering herself. She grasped at her skirt with both hands. "When I heard you had died at the Plaza Hotel, I was in such a state of shock, I couldn't carry out my political duties. I didn't even have an appetite. So when I heard you were alive, I..."

The Seitenshi's lips were pursed tightly, as if trying to hold something back. Then, with her smooth, velvety gloves, she held Rentaro's hands tightly, drawing them toward her.

"I'm so happy you made it, Satomi."

Having such radiant beauty in front of him rendered Rentaro helpless. He let her do as she wished, marveling at how attractive she was up close.

They looked at each other for a long moment—then turned away in unison, blushing. She hid her cheeks with both hands, as if trying to mask the redness.

"I'm sorry... Staring at a man up close like this...this is so improper of me..."

The icy stares of the women behind her made the ruler of Tokyo Area break out in a cold sweat.

"Ex-*cuse* me!" Kisara said, coming between the two and giving the Seitenshi an admonishing look. "Um, L-Lady Seitenshi... I'm not sure you have seen him like this before, so I wanted to give a word of warning: There is *nothing* cool about Satomi at all. He's unintelligent, he's a useless bum, his feet smell, and his face is so ugly that just looking at him drains the energy right out of you."

The Seitenshi rubbed a cheek with her right hand as she gave Kisara an odd look. "Have you and Satomi been seeing each other, President Tendo?"

"We have *not*!"

"Then why do you have such a frantic look on your face?"

"I am *not* frantic at all!" Kisara turned toward Rentaro, as if about to bite him in the neck. "Satomi? One *moment*, please?"

Why's she targeting me?

"So were you just playing around with me, Big Brother?!" Tina wailed.

"Yes! And me, too?!" Enju snapped.

Tina was in a state of abject sadness. Enju was more on the angrier side of the spectrum.

Just as Rentaro was ready to lift his hands in the air and beg for divine intervention, a friendly male voice rang out:

"Oh-ho! The Lady Seitenshi is with you all, too?"

It was a late-middle-aged man with a folded fan, a *hakama* formal skirt, and hair like a pineapple. "Yo!" he said, a greeting well out of character with his traditional garb.

"Mr. Shigaki!" Rentaro shouted, overjoyed at this lifeline thrown to him.

Senichi Shigaki grinned, exposing his white teeth as he guffawed. "I was just thinking that I was overdue for a visit…but oh, my, even Lady Seitenshi has joined the company, has she?"

The Seitenshi gave a well-mannered bow. "Good afternoon to you, Mr. Shigaki. I trust your Varanium mines are faring well?"

"Ha! More or less, I suppose."

"I find it hard to believe that a man who was once Kikunojo's butler has such a talent for business!"

"Ahh, I guess you could say I found my calling late in life, eh? Ha-ha!"

"And I understand you are aiming for electoral office?"

"Oh, you make it sound like such a lofty thing, my Lady! Please, you embarrass me!"

After pleasantries, Shigaki turned to Rentaro and Kisara, flashing them a somewhat distressed smile.

"Kisara," he began, "I…I suppose I owe you an apology, don't I? I'm here because I wanted to do it in person, you see."

Rentaro realized Shigaki was talking about his role in arranging Kisara's would-be marriage.

"I made the arrangements because I thought it would be the best thing for the both of you, but I had no idea young Hitsuma and his father were both caught up in criminal activity. And now look what happened to the young man… Truly, I am sorry."

Kisara gave an open-minded smile at the grown man profusely

apologizing to her. "Not at all," she said. "None of us were hurt, in the end. So don't worry about it, Mr. Shigaki."

"Na-ha-ha! Ah, I thought you might say that."

Rentaro felt a tug at his shirt. Peering down, he found Enju and Tina, concern on their faces as they looked up at him.

"Rentaro, who's that guy?"

"Oh, right, you haven't met him before... Mr. Shigaki?" He motioned to the man, then introduced the trio to one another.

"This is Senichi Shigaki, girls. He's the manager of Tendo Civil Security Agency on paper, and he's also my and Kisara's more-or-less legal guardian."

"Wow! That fancy an old guy, huh?"

"Well! Nice to meet the both of you, then." Shigaki crossed his arms, greeting them with a stern frown at first, then dropping the front and giving them both a friendly pat or two on the head.

"Ah-ha-ha! Would you look at the two cuties we've got here, then? And you know that Shiba girl, too—don't you, Rentaro? Juggling five girls at once! Why, I don't think I managed even *that* many when I was your age, boy!"

Shigaki elbowed Rentaro in the stomach, just in case his point hadn't come across clearly enough. But before Rentaro could yelp *Sir, no, I—*, the elbow knocked the coffee out of his hands. It went flying through the air, the still-hot liquid arcing dangerously toward the sleeve of Shigaki's jacket—

By the time Rentaro thought *Oh crap*, it was already too late.

"Yeowch!"

Shigaki went to a knee, lifting up his sleeve in an attempt to dodge. Rentaro rushed to him, social shame overcoming him as Shigaki took out a handkerchief and lowered his sleeve again. The old man's eyes were aimed squarely at Rentaro's coffee cup. "What on earth, my boy? It's hot as blazes out here, and you're going around with hot coffee in your hand? What's that all about, hmm? Is that what's popular with the young folks these days?"

"I, um, you aren't burned or anything, sir?"

"Mm?" Shigaki nonchalantly replied. "Ahh, this'll be fine."

"Let's go up to the office," Tina suggested. "We've got some cold water up there."

Shigaki gave it a moment's thought, then agreed to stop by long enough to use the sink. *This is sure turning into a weird day*, Rentaro thought as he accompanied his legal guardian up the stairs and inside.

Enju, watching from behind as Tina and Rentaro escorted Shigaki, was nailed to the ground in surprise. She crossed her arms, wondering what all that was about.

Apparently she was the only one out of the group who noticed, but when Shigaki had his sleeve lifted up for that split-second, she saw something.

He must have been a fan of tattoos, because he had something that looked like one on his upper arm. Kind of a fancy design, too—a pentagram with wings on top of all five points. It was an odd mismatch with his otherwise conservative choice of wardrobe.

But Enju was never one to dwell on things too long. Kicking the observation out of her ever-curious mind, she darted up the stairs after Rentaro.

Senichi Shigaki, having safely made his fortune in the Varanium mining industry, owned a house in one of the poshest areas of Tokyo Area's District 1. Inside the large residence, within a study that he forbade anyone else to enter, there was a bookcase half-recessed in the wall, one filled with old classics and dictionaries patiently waiting to be opened again.

If someone with architectural experience entered this study after giving the house an examination from the outside, he or she probably would have noticed that the room was far too small compared to the external dimensions.

Upon returning to this study, Shigaki turned not toward the handsome mahogany desk resting on one side of the room, but to the far end of this bookcase. He took out *The Encyclopedic Guide to Weapons of the World, Vol. 3*, then inserted a key into the hole that lurked behind the tome. This activated the Elecompack-branded mobile shelving. The shelf, laden with books, glided along rails on the floor.

In an instant, the wall of books had fallen back, revealing a corridor to a new room.

With a practiced gait, Shigaki delved into the pitch-black hall and the inscrutable abyss. The dimensions of the space were only barely visible.

Then, out of nowhere, there was the *whoosh* of flame springing to life, followed by the floor lighting up a dim shade of blue.

It illuminated a large leather executive chair, which Shigaki promptly used. That was enough to energize the light, instantly brightening the entire room. A pentagram drew itself on the floor, adding intricately designed wings to each point with a single stroke.

"You're late, you idiot. You think you've got enough clout with this group to keep *me* waiting?"

Looking up, Shigaki saw an executive chair much like his own at one of the star's vertices. There sat a man with his legs crossed, his bushy beard and head of hair giving him the appearance of a lion. It was Sougen Saitake, the lone Five Wings Syndicate executive manager from Osaka.

Shigaki, Tokyo Area's top manager, looked around the room. As far as he could see, only two points on the pentagram were occupied—his and Saitake's. The other three chairs were empty.

"I suppose I can excuse Hokkaido for its absence, but where's Hakata and Sendai?"

"How should I know? I'm fine with just the two of us handling everything, regardless."

Looking closer at Saitake revealed that his body had a blue-tinged light coursing around it—the telltale sign of a holographic broadcast.

Shigaki was attending nothing less than a board meeting. One attended by the five most powerful people in Five Wings—the chosen vertices of the pentagram.

"I have just returned," Shigaki solemnly began, "from a meeting with Rentaro and his people. The sheer enormity of what he destroyed, and yet he couldn't have been more carefree with me."

"Yes, I'm sure having your contacts purged from the police force must have been quite a setback."

"Not exactly. We can replace them all anytime we like. If you call *that* a 'setback,' I think having a certain someone send an undercover assassin over to kill the Seitenshi was rather more of a setback for our cause, was it not?"

"Ah." Saitake stared into space, looking somewhat embarrassed. "I am glad to see your snide remarks haven't suffered at all. I thought eliminating the Seitenshi would be the most efficient way to move things along. I gave you all an ultimatum. You responded with this naive idealism, so I went through with it. You know full well that I have no time for those kind of people. Either you follow me, or you get the hell out of my way. That's how I do business."

"Saitake, you have no idea how Tokyo Area works. The Seitenshi is an indispensable symbol—government personified. We need her if the Area's government is to retain any kind of public mandate. The chaos that would result from her killing could help us come to power, yes, but as long as the Tendo family has not been toppled, any effect would be fleeting at best. We have to get Kikunojo Tendo out of the picture first."

"And that's why you're going through the incredibly circuitous route of securing Kisara Tendo? Shigaki, is that girl truly worth all this effort?"

Shigaki shook his head. Of *course* he had to bring that up. "You didn't see the crime-scene photographs of Kazumitsu Tendo's murder. You wouldn't understand until you do. That girl is the most demonic offspring the Tendo clan has ever seen."

"Oh?"

"Plus, I understand *her* ultimate goal is to kill Kikunojo Tendo as well. We both seek the same thing."

"Hmph. And yet you failed to recruit her."

"Oh, I've quite succeeded."

"Mm?"

Shigaki's lips curled.

"I said, I've succeeded."

Saitake fell silent, attempting to gauge how true this was.

"By the way," Shigaki continued, "how is Juzouji doing?"

"Hmph. The machine's purring along, you could say. He thought you were the number-two of the group after me, you'll be delighted to know."

"Ha! You'll be taking my 'snide' crown from me before long, you know."

"Only because I've learned from the best."

The two chuckled at each other across the darkness.

"So," Saitake said, "Five Wings has taken the leadership posts of Osaka Area and Hokkaido Area. We have three left to go. Do not let our dream escape your memory. Our cause is just."

"Glory to the Five Wings."

"Glory to the Five Wings."

The blue light disappeared. The room was wrapped in darkness once more.

The howl of a lonely dog echoed from some faraway point. The darkness was growing thicker as Rentaro Satomi dragged his sore feet across the brightly lit street, on his way back home. The smell of burnt explosives pervading his body gave him a headache; his arms were shaking so bad from all the recoil he was surprised nothing had gotten dislocated. Using chopsticks might pose a challenge for him later on.

He tried putting his hands over both ears, but the ringing continued. It was a pretty bad case. He had working ear protectors on—or, at least, they were supposed to be working; Miori's new gun and ammunition must have generated too much of an explosive blast for them.

He had spent the entire past day running testing duty for Shiba Heavy Weapons' latest products. Miori was busy developing a handgun that used powerful Initiator-specific ammo. Once it was complete, he was planning to ask Miori for the first one off the line so he could hand it to Tina.

Miori never said anything about Rentaro's recent legal trouble. The closest she got to that was when she said, "Time to pay me back, Satomi dear," after passing him at the gun range. It was just more of that weird sense of distance she liked to retain with him. He kind of liked it.

He was busy enjoying the sense of fatigue that racked his body as he tromped up the metal stairway and turned the doorknob to his apartment. The moment he opened it up, he was greeted by a girl in a black sailor-style school uniform and a frilly apron.

"Welcome back, Satomi."

"Um…Kisara?"

She was all smiles, going behind Rentaro and pushing him into the room. He took off his jacket and loosened his necktie as he looked around. Then he realized the other girls in his life weren't there.

"Where's Enju and Tina?"

"They're out watching the neighborhood fireworks show."

Rentaro slapped a hand with his fist. "Oh! The one where they ask you to pay five hundred yen to join the district association? That was today?"

Five hundred yen didn't seem like it'd be enough to result in all that exciting a show, but the girls had yet to see any kind of fireworks this year. They were willing to bite at just about anything.

Kisara, reading Rentaro's face, gently shook her head. "Oh, it's fine. You have to be twelve or younger to participate, anyway. They'll have a bigger show at the main festival soon enough. We can all hit that one together."

Huh. So this is the first night I'll be alone with Kisara in a while, then.

Rentaro noticed the assortment of colorful dishes on the low table. He could tell she had been using the kitchen. An ever so slightly foul smell wafted in from somewhere. The nervous sweats were coming already.

"Kisara, you didn't…cook, did you?"

She smiled in response. Instead of answering, she simply pointed two thumbs at herself. She must have had nearly ten bandages wrapped around her fingers.

"Well," she said, "it's kind of annoying to have everyone pick on my food all the time, you know? I'm trying to improve a little bit."

Rentaro flung his body down by the table, admitting defeat in the face of Kisara's *mangia, mangia* aura.

An acrid, sour stench, like the contents of a dog's stomach freshly unfurled on the carpet, stung his nostrils. "Oh, God," he whispered, shutting his eyes tight.

The gel-like piece of organic matter on the plate ferried from the kitchen was done up in a horrid array of colors, like a crazed painter splattering a canvas with everything he had on his palette. Just looking at it gave Rentaro a crash course on what insanity truly meant.

The smell it emitted stabbed into his eyes. He tried to pass it off to Kisara as tears of joy while he scooped up a bit in the spoon. It was oddly springy, jiggling about in excitement. With one final, resigned motion, he brought it to his mouth.

For a single moment, he experienced nirvana. Across the river, he could see his father, Takaharu Satomi, beckoning at him.

"Gehh, this slop is disgu—"

"Dis-guh-*what*?" Kisara stared daggers into his eyes.

"It's one of the most alarming creations of mankind!"

"Ooh, tell me more."

"It's like the food of some mad artist! It makes my very pulse stop!"

"Hee-hee! Thank you."

Kisara, luckily, was stupid enough not to realize she wasn't being complimented.

"—Stop treating me like an idiot!"

—Or not. He was hoping to string her along a bit longer than *that*, at least. His roommate stood up in a huff, running a hand distractedly through her hair.

"Ugghh, I just… All right, *you* teach me, Satomi."

"Huh?"

Suddenly, Kisara was bashful, toes almost turned inward as she rubbed her thighs together.

"Satomi, you promised you'd teach me how to cook, didn't you? Before all…*that* happened. Like, when we had those sweet potatoes?"

Oh. Right. He *did* say that to her. Maybe.

After a moment's thought, he stood and rolled up his sleeves. "All right, whaddaya want to make?"

"…What's the secret to your stir-fried vegetables?"

There wasn't any "secret" to it. Vegetables, pan, oil, *bam*. But Kisara was ready to go, tightening her apron and chopping up some spinach from the fridge. Rentaro stood behind her in the director's role. Or he meant to. But after just a couple minutes, he already couldn't stand it any longer, taking her hands from behind.

They had to begin with how to use a kitchen knife. The knife tapped several times unsteadily against the chopping board. The TV wasn't on. Several quiet moments passed.

"Um, Kisara?"

"Hmm?"

"Did you...like Hitsuma, or anything?"

Kisara silently kept her hands moving. The *tap-tap* continued swiftly.

Silence reigned for several moments. It was painful.

"I don't know."

"Oh..."

"But I don't think it was love, or anything."

"...You kissed him, though, didn't you?"

Rentaro cursed himself. He should've known when to give up, and he didn't. But the panic on Kisara's face as she opened her eyes wide and said, "You saw that...?" was far greater than his.

"N-no!" she continued. "Not like that. I kind of had my palm up like this, to block it, and when Hitsuma came up to me, I kind of pushed..."

She must have realized she wasn't being very convincing with her little hand-gesture show. Kisara tried desperately to figure out how to win Rentaro's trust—but then he smiled at her. Paradoxically enough, seeing her act so serious convinced him that all his worries were for nothing.

"He...he didn't do anything like what you're thinking, Satomi. So I'm still a...a virgin and everything, too..."

"Uh, yeah."

Something about the sudden introduction of bedroom terminology made Rentaro's pulse quicken as he added salad oil to the frying pan and put the spinach on top. It shrank down with an audible sizzle.

"So, speaking of which, did you hear about the new prime minister of Hokkaido Area?"

He thought he was being ignored for a moment before Kisara softly replied. "Yeah, what a surprise. Pretty amazing, huh? Prime Minister Kiryu was fine one day, and then...poof."

Both Rentaro and Kisara had met him several times during their time at the Tendo mansion. "Yeah, I was pretty shocked, too," he added. "I figured he was gonna serve in that post until he was one hundred or so."

"Did you hear the rumor, though?"

"What?"

"I heard that Kiryu ate breakfast, then started clutching his chest out of nowhere and fell off his chair. He never woke up after that. Like, apparently they found a lot of weird things during the autopsy, too. Supposedly they wanted to do some more testing on the body, but it got blocked and they reported it as death from illness. They closed up the whole investigation before it began."

"The hell?" Rentaro asked, taken aback.

Kisara replied with a lifeless shaking of her head. "I don't know."

"You think the new prime minister's an okay guy? Tsukihiko Juzouji?"

"They say he's pretty sharp. He's probably up to the job, I guess."

Rentaro felt conflicted. He wasn't really a fan of Souichi Kiryu's style of governing. He always acted so self-righteous and arrogant in front of the cameras, like he thrived on public controversy. But maybe that was the kind of leadership it took to guide the island of Hokkaido from postwar ruin to a rebuilt local power in the course of a single generation. Either way, few actively cheered for his passing.

Plain spinach sauté was a little lacking by itself, so with Kisara's permission, he filled a kettle with water and placed it on an adjacent burner. He turned the knob, and heat, along with the smell of gas, wafted as the blue flame ignited.

She worked her cooking chopsticks. The sizzling continued. In his role as teacher, Rentaro was giving Kisara instructions from behind her back. To an impartial observer, however, it might have looked like they were embracing each other.

Her hair smelled good. The apron looked good over her uniform, he thought.

"Hey, actually, Kisara, why do you always have some kind of uniform on? Are you trying to match me or something?"

"Because I can use it as workwear. It keeps me from having to change between here and school. I have my own clothes, too, but probably not as much as most girls my age. Probably a *hell* of a lot less, actually."

There was something boastful, downright haughty, about the way she accented the *hell* in that sentence. It was like she was trying to put pressure on Rentaro with it. He scratched the back of his head as he stared off into the distance.

"Uh, you wanna maybe go clothes shopping sometime?"

"Ohhh? Sure. I'll try to develop some expensive tastes between now and then."

She brought a hand to her hip, lightly, as if she was about to start whistling with glee. Her short skirt swayed a bit in response.

"B-but," a stammering Rentaro continued, "I just mean... You looked great in that kimono for the meet up, and you looked great in that wedding dress, too, but... Really, I think you look the best when you're in that black uniform, in the end. I mean it. You're beautiful."

Kisara turned around. Her eyes were wide.

Why does love always have to be this asymmetrical thing? Every time, there seems to be this imbalance between everything I feel about someone else, and everything she thinks about me. The scales always tip one way or the other. What do I have to do to bring the ache in my heart across to her?

His voice failed him. It frustrated him immensely. Whenever he was in front of someone he liked, his vocal abilities plummeted to the point where he wanted to die.

Instead of relying on them, he took a step forward.

"K-Kisara!"

He brought his hand around her narrow waist, clutching it tight. Kisara's chest pushed up to him with a yelp. Her unbelievably well-built face was right next to his, a sweet aroma filling his nostrils.

Her cheeks grew more and more flush. Her own heat was stirring a little.

"Whoa, hey, Satomi, where're you—?"

"—Back at the visitation room..."

"Huh?"

Rentaro tilted his head down and brought his lips to Kisara's ear.

"When I berated you and ordered you out of the room... I'm truly sorry. I was such an idiot that whole time. I never should have said any of that to you. I know I'm late saying this, but I'm so, so happy to be home. Thank you, Kisara."

The edges of the surprised Kisara's wide-open eyes filled with an onrush of transparent liquid. A single line ran across one cheek. She wiped at it with a knuckle. Then her broad eyebrows arched up as she looked at Rentaro, eyes soft and gentle. The tears were from a happy place. He could tell.

"Don't be stupid. I was waiting for you to say that the whole time."

"Kisara…"

The joy upon hearing this drove the elated Rentaro to bring his face closer. Kisara turned away, her face red from ear to ear.

"W-wait, Satomi. I really can't do…that… I'm too embar… I'll die if I…"

At any other time, Rentaro would have respected Kisara's wishes and taken a step back. But now, Rentaro was tired. Tired of writhing under an agony he had no answer for. Even if it meant his destruction, he could no longer hold it in. He had to see where it finally led him.

Rentaro relaxed his grip slightly.

"Well, if you really don't want to, Kisara, I'll stop right now."

"Really?"

"No," he said in her ear as he brought their lips together.

The kettle began to whistle.

With a clank, her cooking chopsticks fell to the floor.

Sumire had been right all along: *"If you really just want Kisara to be happy, you're gonna have to keep killing off your own feelings. There's no way to half-ass that. Do you swear you'll do that?"*

And now Rentaro had broken his promise.

Nothing about his outlook had changed. Marrying Hitsuma had been the only way for Kisara to forget about revenge and live out her life. It had been the sole, and final, method for her to move on. Even if that had meant Rentaro would have had to abandon his love forever—if that had led to Tendo no longer feeling compelled to massacre her own family, he would've had to accept that. But *now* he knew:

Being in love was like insanity.

Rentaro was insane for Kisara. He was awash in love, inflamed by it. And he couldn't stop her revenge any longer. This love had every indication of taking the entire world down with it.

At the last possible moment, Rentaro had taken the selfish route. He would be forced to pay for that sometime, no doubt. He would probably regret it. Regret that, except for this single moment, he could never stop Kisara.

He had resolved to fight for the sake of "justice." It could drive him, someday in the future, to cross paths with Kisara and the "absolute evil" that flowed in her. There was no way he could deny that.

Soon, Kisara would be taking sword in hand to hunt down the Tendo family, her sworn nemeses. With every one she slashed down, the rift between her and Rentaro would grow that much wider. There may never be another sweet day like this one in their lives together. Perhaps this was the peak. Perhaps, after this, they'd both come tumbling down, their mutual hatred piling up on itself as they did.

But—

No matter how much their relationship deteriorated from now on, no matter how much they screamed at and harangued each other, no matter how much they stabbed at each other with their blades of loathing—for now, *now* at least, he wanted to give up his body to her soft lips.

He pushed Kisara against the refrigerator and forcefully locked his lips against hers. The soft valleys of Kisara's chest pushed against him. They softly flattened down, changing shape. Her eyes narrowed, as if she was intoxicated by these events, and she brought her hands around Rentaro's neck.

He was willing to do anything to leave his body to the bliss that lay ahead, but Sumire's voice refused to let go of his mind:

"You can always rebuild a broken body, but a broken heart's beyond all help. You can't do a thing with it.

"And if it's too late for Kisara, that's gonna be up to you to manage."

- Enju Aihara has a Gastrea Virus corrosion rate of 43.8%
- An estimated 496 days left until shape collapse

AFTERWORD

Black Bullet is officially being made into an anime! Thanks to all of you for your support!

...Although, to be honest, I'm a bit torn. Should I really be so unreserved in my happiness at this? After all, I devoted myself heart and soul to make this the most exciting piece of text I could. Will my book remain entertaining in other media formats? As I write this, at least, I'm having a little trouble imagining how it'll work out.

However, the anime team members I've met have all been masters of their craft—super passionate about their work, but also coolly analytical of what it takes to make this happen. I'm sure I'll start bragging about this project a lot more as I get to learn about them and the values that drive them more, but already there's no doubt in my mind that I can leave my brainchild safely in their hands.

We have half a year before the TV broadcast begins. Specialists from a wealth of different fields will be coming together, pooling their talents and working hard to make this as high quality a production as they can. Will the *Black Bullet* anime be worth the [digital] cels it's drawn on? It's up to all of you, the viewers, to watch and judge the results for yourselves.

I hope you'll give the anime as warm a welcome as possible.

My thanks go out once again to Mr. Kurosaki, my editor. Even as the threat of this book slipping loomed larger and louder than ever before, the constant smile he wore as he worked from start to finish made even the deepest cauldron of hell feel like a dip in the ocean by comparison. They also go out to my illustrator Saki Ukai, whose ESP abilities apparently allow him to figure out which way is north at any time. Also thanks to Mr. Kojima, director of the anime project, and everybody under his command, as well as the producers, Mr. Ogura and Mr. Ogasawara. Finally, I want to thank everybody in the editorial team and elsewhere who helped bring this book to life.

Finally, a note to my readers. Not to go sharing my personal life with you, but around three years ago, when I first joined the Dengeki publishing family, I had a conversation with Mr. Kurosaki along the lines of "I'm gonna sell a million copies and get an anime version released!"—a conversation very much along the lines of what the manga *Bakuman* depicted. I didn't sweat the details too much at the time, and the declaration was made less for me than for Mr. Kurosawa (who had just transferred into that department back then). Still, one of those two goals is now a reality. I really have all of you to thank for keeping me from being a complete liar. Again, thank you.

Regardless of how the anime turns out, however, the novels can't afford to play second fiddle. My focus now is producing a series that'll make people who took in all three versions—novel, manga, anime—think to themselves, *They were all good, but the novels are what really hit it out of the park!*

Thank you very much for taking this novel in hand. May all the blessings of God rain down upon all my readers.

Shiden Kanzaki